MATED TO TEAM SHADOW

A REVERSE HAREM PARANORMAL ROMANCE

JADE ALTERS

JEANINE

The party pitched to full swing, and the revelers were too sloppy drunk or high to pay attention to my movements. This allowed me to poke my nose in places where it did not belong. The only people I had to watch were the four ridiculously smoking hot bodyguards dressed in black from shoulder to toe stationed throughout the yacht.

But although I acted as loopy as the tanned and toned high rollers surrounding Aedan Morgan, I could pick out a path to his office. Here I hoped to find the clue to my old college roommate's fate. At the very least, I might find convincing evidence about her kidnapping and/or Morgan's nefarious deeds.

When I use the word "nefarious," it's for good reason. Interpol suspected Morgan was the kingpin of not only drug running but Caribbean piracy. This last scored high on the law enforcement's radar because a frightening surge of pirate attacks plagued Latin America and the Caribbean last year. Law enforcement recorded seventy-one pirate attacks in the area—a one hundred and sixty-three percent increase from the previous year. Morgan certainly had a piece of that.

But no one could make a case against the elusive Morgan. The pirate playing the part of an international playboy gave the bastard plenty of cover and ability to move about the cabin, figuratively. Last I saw, Morgan sat immobile on the upper deck in a half-conscious state after sucking in several lines of pearly white coke.

It must be good to be a criminal mastermind. At least he lived well enough. The yacht, surreptitiously renamed the *Lady E*, was gorgeous though only worth thirteen million dollars. Higher-end floating palaces go for thirty-eight mil and more, but I guessed beggars couldn't be choosers when you procured your watercraft through theft. Highly polished walnut panels lined the walls, and the hallway floors had the softest carpet I'd ever felt. Yeah, I must check my bank account to see if I had thirteen mil to cover the price of one of these babies.

As if.

Newsflash. Investigative journalists beginning their careers do not make big bucks.

I smoothed my gold sequined mini-dress scored at a New York designer's showroom at a deep discount. It was not an outfit I'd normally buy. The cut dipped too low and the hem too high, but it purchased me entrée into many venues that demanded a particular cache for admittance.

At once trashy and expensive, it pegged me as the type of party girl welcomed into the dens of iniquity of the rich and famous. I checked my stylish blonde bob wig, stolen from my mother's inventory, to make sure it was in place. Then I moved forward, zig-zagging through the partygoers carefully to support the illusion I was drunk. If they caught me, I needed a plausible excuse why I veered off course.

So much depended on me not getting caught.

"Où est... salle de bain?" I said in my sloppy French, to the immobile bodyguard stationed at the doorway that led to the staterooms and Morgan's office.

He stared at me with animal dispassion as if I were prey, and I shivered. His nostrils flared, but other than that, not a single muscle twitched on his classically chiseled face.

Down girl, I thought. *You are not here to play.* Though if I were, Mr. Tall, Dark and Dangerous would tick the right boxes. Chalk it up to my intrepid and impulsive nature, but I have yet to meet an inappropriate man I'm not drawn to.

Which was why I remained steadfastly single. Still, his high cheeks, his classic straight nose, square jaw, wide shoulders and ripped abs that did *not* hide behind his black sweater whispered to me, "*Come here, little darling.*"

"The head," he replied in English, "is down the hall, second door on the right."

Head. Interesting choice of words. Marines use that term for the bathroom.

"*Merci,*" I said, and then realized I announced I understood English. *Hell. I hope I haven't blown my cover.* But I reassured myself speaking more than one language was common in most parts of the world. In contrast to the United States where it was nearly a cultural crime to know more than one language.

I fake stumbled forward and then found myself thrown into the bodyguard's solid form by a bona fide impaired guest making for the same accommodation.

"Sorry," the guest slurred, and staggered past us.

"*Excuze-moi,*" I said as the delicious bodyguard caught me in his strong arms. His scent intoxicated me with an enticing mix of sandalwood and musk.

He bent to my ear and whispered, "You can cut the bull-shit French. You sound like a boarding school reject."

I pushed away with more force than my supposedly drunk condition would have allowed and glared at him.

"There is no need to be insulting," I said. "Sometimes you have to lay it on thick to get into these parties."

"Oh, I'm sure you lay something," he said with a curled lip.

"*Va te faire foutre,*" I snapped. But telling the man to kiss my ass didn't illicit even a twitch.

He cocked his head. "Sorry. On duty. Better run along now. The gentleman has finished." His head snapped to level his gaze on the rowdy crowd. Dismissed, I stepped away stewing at his rude treatment until I realized the bodyguard announced the man finished before he opened the door.

Arrogant son-of-a-bitch.

I passed the drunk and slid open the door. Instead of walking inside, I looked over my shoulder to check that the bodyguard had his eyes on his paper watching the crowd. I slid it shut and tiptoed down the hall and slipped in the door I'd spotted Morgan walking from earlier.

The stateroom featured a large wood desk before an immense porthole that was more a wide pane of glass than hole looking over the St. Lucia harbor. Lights from the town sparkled in the bluish light of deep evening, seeming more like a fairyland than bustling port. We were gliding toward a slip, a sure sign the evening was about to come to a close and announced my narrowing window of opportunity.

I glanced around the cabin frustrated by the pristine cleanliness of its occupant. Who would think that an international criminal had a clean fetish? I walked to the desk and rattled each drawer to find them locked tight.

Merde.

I was not without resources, just a rapidly dwindling amount of time for my investigation. I pulled the metal nail file I hid in my bra and worked the lock of the topmost long, thin, middle drawer. This is the place where many people kept sensitive information on thumb drives.

The question was whether Morgan could be counted on to be like other people, in any respect. I had to hope so because I found no other place he could hide information.

My misspent youth hassling the principal of my high school rewarded me with a click. Heart thudding, I pulled open the desk to find a leather journal and several thumb drives.

Score!

I hope.

I pried open the leather journal to find it was a ledger with words and numbers but in Spanish. Since my Spanish was as good as my French, I couldn't make heads or tails of the words. I slipped my iPhone SE from my bra, stripped of all apps and not connected to a service. Its use was strictly to take photographs, and its compact size made it easier to conceal in clothing. I worked to steady my shaking hands as I snapped sharp photos of the pages. The ship shuddered from a bump which I could only surmise was the dock.

I was officially out of time.

One more shot and I'd have captured the written pages. I slipped the phone back into my bra. In a scorching second of bravado and heedless of the danger, I scooped up the thumb drives and stuffed them in my bra, determined I would get off this vessel before Morgan discovered the drives missing.

Or so I hoped.

The cabin door rattled, and my heart nearly stopped as I shoved the desk drawer closed.

The door flew open revealing a bodyguard. Only he wasn't tall and dark. He stood delectably tall, buff, and blond.

"Who are you?" he said with his eyes narrowed.

"I'm looking for the bathroom," I said sloppily, aiming to pull off my drunk act.

His eyes narrowed because he clearly did not believe me.

His nostrils flared too and surprise lit his handsome green eyes. The bodyguard touched a headset on his ear.

"Intruder in the primary's office."

He nodded and touched the headset again.

"Roger," he said.

My stomach fluttered with a thousand nervous butterflies, and as usual in dangerous conditions, I now needed to use the bathroom, but I had to hold it.

"Oh, baby," I said in a seductive voice. "I didn't mean to make any trouble. I'll just go on my way."

But Tall, Blonde and Delicious wasn't having it as he moved to the desk, and I tried to pass by him. He grabbed my arm in a viselike grip and stopped my forward motion cold.

"Wait here," he said with utter politeness as if he was a waiter offering a menu.

"I should go," I said.

"No," said a rougher voice. Another of the bodyguards stood in the door. And this one was massive. He had to turn to get his expansive shoulders into the cabin. His deep blue eyes stared into me to the divine secrets of my soul. His nostrils flared too.

What is it with these guys flaring their nostrils?

"What do we have here?" said another voice.

Morgan came up behind the bodyguard, standing straight and utterly sober in his white linen suit. The bastard had played us all. The butterflies in my stomach morphed to big nasty moths seeking escape as suspicion glittered in his cold eyes. My heart sank as I realized that he did not buy my drunk act.

"Gunner found her here," said the big guy.

Morgan sauntered past both bodyguards.

"Find something of interest?" he said with an oily voice. I imagined a snake sliding across my skin, and I shivered.

"I was looking for the bathroom," I said.

"And found my desk instead. Let's see." He slid around the desk and pulled at the middle drawer, that I'd left unlocked. It sprung open, incriminatingly. Inwardly I cringed.

"Hmm," he said. Morgan glanced at the biggest guard. "Frisk her," he said.

I looked to Morgan and to the guards and did the math. If I didn't find a way out of here, I would disappear as easily as my friend Surma.

Tall, blonde and delicious, AKA Gunner, responded to a flick of Big Guy's head and advanced on me. I shrunk against the bulkhead and desperately searched for an out. Toeing off my sandals, I scanned the distance between my position and the door. I had to hope I had surprise and speed on my side.

I curled my body then leaped to put one foot on the desk. I jumped forward to sail past the black-garbed muscle, landed and rolled. Three years of high school gymnastics paid off at odd times, like this one. I stood and sprinted into the hallway only to run into another six-foot mountain of muscle, and he stared at me in amusement as I bounced off him.

"Grab her," said Gunner.

"We don't have time for this," said Big Guy.

"Yeah, but we can't leave her behind," said Gunner.

"Are all the guests off the ship?"

"Yes, Ryker," said the guy in the hall.

"And the crew?"

"Gave them shore leave. It thrilled them."

"Where's Damon?" said Ryker.

"Here, boss," said Tall, Dark, and Dangerous, AKA Damon.

"Let's hit it then," said Ryker. "Grab her, Gunner."

"With pleasure, Ryker." Unceremoniously, Gunner threw me over his shoulder.

"Wait," said Morgan coming from the stateroom. "What's going on?"

"We're terminating our employment," said Ryker.

As he finished speaking, a sun-splitting boom rocked the ship.

RYKER

The C-4 blast thundered through the ship, and the shockwave of the timed explosions threw us against the deck. Gunner had placed the first charge at the bow of the yacht for Morgan's benefit. But damn it, that pirate was in the wrong place, courtesy of Gunner failing to man his assigned position. He should have kept Morgan cornered until the last minute.

"Fuck!" sputtered Morgan. As he tried to stand, the second explosion splayed him across the bulkhead.

"Who are you guys?" the pirate rumbled with a dangerous tone in his voice.

"No time for chit-chat. Adios."

I eyed my team. "Go! Go! Go!" I yelled. The four of us with our guest scrambled toward the ladder that would take us below deck where the auxiliary watercraft sat. That was the plan: Get in, set the charges, steal—I mean, appropriate the speedboat and watch one slime-ball go up in flames.

The woman bounced on Gunner's shoulder spitting fury and beating his shoulders.

Too damn bad. Serves Gunner right.

"Did you unleash the moorings, Kane?"

He nodded grimly, and we moved forward with uneven steps. The ship listed to the side, toward the water and away from the dock, hampering our progress. Gunner had placed the charges this way purposefully, we didn't want to damage the dock.

We crawled through the skewed hallway to the ladder that would bring us to the lowest deck where Morgan stored the yacht's powerboat. Our getaway plan required to speedboat; we couldn't afford to put our feet on foreign soil. Without passports and involved in a dubious operation, we couldn't count on recovery. This was strictly a "disavow any knowledge" mission, meaning that until we got into international waters, we were on our own.

Damon growled beside me. His frustration rolled over him because he knew what I would say.

"No. Not here," I said.

"Why the fuck not?"

I jerked my head toward the woman Gunner slung over his shoulder.

"Not in front of the normals."

"Damn, Gunner."

Once at the ladder, show-off Damon jumped to the lower deck. He held open his hands.

"Toss her here, Gunner."

"Toss?" she squeaked.

"Sure enough, but I get her back."

Gunner pulled her off his shoulder and dropped her feet-first as she screamed. But Damon scooped her up and thrust her into my arms. One by one our boots thudded on the metal deck, while Kane and Damon raced to push the boat into the water. Fortunately, our forced rearrangement of the yacht's hull brought the water level to the power boat's keel. However, we'd have to hurry, or we wouldn't clear the rapidly sinking opening at the stern to make our getaway. The sharp and acrid smell of diesel alerted me that at least one of the fuel tanks had ruptured, making it even more imperative that we get out of Dodge.

Gunner dropped the woman in the boat, and I stayed behind to shove the craft and ensure it cleared the sinking yacht. Damon started the engine. The glub sound of the engine almost reassured me that we'd get away clean. But the yacht listed again, and only inches remained to push the boat through the opening.

"Go!" I yelled as I ran along the side pushing, determined to make the boat squeeze through at an angle. Damon steered the sleek speedboat forward and put it in gear.

"Keep going!" I yelled again, and his expression hardened because he knew he'd be leaving me behind. We worked on the buddy system to cover each other's backs. Damon was my go-to, but I made an executive decision for their safety over mine. Damon grimaced, disliking my decision, but he accelerated and piloted the boat to clear water.

The yacht groaned and listed submerging the opening in seconds while the shell of the ceiling hovered inches above my head. Gear lining the walls of the boat bay floated in the rapidly narrowing gap. The lights flickered and snuffed, casting me in darkness. I needed out before I became a casualty. I knew better than to panic, but adrenaline pumped through me.

I jumped into the water, and the ocean surrounded me, its liquid Caribbean warmth saturating my clothes, pulling me down. With hours of training and experience kept the panic at bay momentarily, but with the ship submerging fast, my heart pounded thinking this vessel could be my coffin. I swam toward where I believed the opening should be, but it alluded me. Diesel in the water clouded my vision, and my hands couldn't find the egress to the open water.

From training, I knew I could hold my breath for three minutes, but that wouldn't be enough time to locate the opening and then reach the surface.

Either I took extreme measures, or I was toast. And it would be ironic and a shame for a Navy SEAL to drown. Not that it hadn't happened before, but I was adamant it would not be me. I'd be damned if I let Davy Jones' locker take me.

Rising into the air pocket, I took a lungful of air and started the change. The burn began along my spine and spread to my legs, rearranging them from arms and legs into the limbs of a four-legged beast. My face elongated and my eyes and ears moved to different places. I sensed an opening underwater, as my jaguar ears caught sounds that my human ears could not, and my eyes saw flashes of movement obscured to me in human form. I sucked in a deep breath and dove, letting the rumbles, pops, and pings of the power-boat lead me to open water. As a human, this would have been impossible. As my animal self, it was easier than eating a candy bar.

The shift meant I'd lost my clothes but it was a small price to pay for my life. Freed, I paddled through the water. .

The rumble of the power boat's engine grew louder, so I knew Damon had stopped her and waited for me to show. I poked my head up and roared to let my team know I was nearby, then I dove and shifted back to my human form. The sea water held me in its warm embrace while my bones realigned. Once limbs had become arms and legs, and my fur receded, I broke the surface of the water and waved.

The men appeared relieved, but they should know I'd always find a way.

I swam to the boat and Kane reached his arm toward the water to help me up into the boat. The woman's eyes grew wide at my naked state and Gunner threw a towel at me which I wrapped around my waist.

"My eyes," he whined with one of his stupid jokes.

Then Kane and Damon smiled, but it was more from relief that we'd all gotten out alive.

"Boss," said Damon as he peered over his shoulder. "We have incoming."

I swiveled my head to see a St. Lucia Coast Guard cutter heading our way. But it was an aging vessel and wouldn't match the power of this demon of the seas.

We'd chosen St. Lucia for this reason, and also because politically, they didn't mind assassinating known criminals. Their campaigns painted the island as a safe haven, carefully policed, to make it more attractive to tourists. When Damon told me, I nearly woofed my beer. St. Lucia? An eye-catching little island nation whose local law enforcement commanded the naval forces? It was an extreme solution for a tiny country. Still, we did not want to be caught by them or to have to explain why United States' SEALS were in their sovereign waters.

Damon revved the engines with a roar, and the 260-horsepower engine pulled ahead, leaving the cutter and St. Lucia a brief memory in a hopefully long life.

"How did we do?" I asked. The repeated slaps of the boat on the surface of the ocean forced me to sit, which I did next to our passenger.

"The bastard got to the dock," said Kane grimly.

"We shot. We didn't score," opined Gunner sourly. "What's Plan B?"

I needed to chew out the entire team, especially Gunner, but I was aware our guest barely clung to the bench as she shivered. She'd put up a brave front so far, but people handled stress in different ways. The last thing she needed was a Marine Sargent yelling at her.

"Alpha-Mike-Foxtrot. Time to disavow all of you and head to a nice island off the south of France."

"No can do, boss man, you can't adios us until the objective is achieved."

"How about we get our passenger to safety then and not spill mission objectives in front of civilians?"

"You've," she said, "failed in that."

I stared at her and couldn't pull my gaze away. Her eyes were the color of both sand and sea, two of my very favorite things, and her hair—wait. It glinted artificially in the sun, and something about the way it smelled confused me.

I yanked the wig off her head.

"Hey!"

Yeah, I got it now. Another woman's scent clung to the wig. I tossed it into the water.

"That belonged to my mother."

"Then why was it on your head?"

"None of your business," she snapped.

"Get her phone," said Gunner, "and the jump drives she stuffed in her bra."

"How do you—" she said indignantly.

"Sweetie, you were bouncing on my shoulder. I felt them."

"Oh, a regular princess and the pea," she snapped.

Damon chuckled over his shoulder, and Kane joined him. "That's a good name for you, Gunner. I like it," said Damon. "Princess."

"Don't you fucking dare, Darkman."

"You gonna make me?"

"Boy, boys," I said with my best authoritative air. "Let's not scare the lady with your juvenile antics."

"By all means," she said. "Let's frighten me with kidnapping and talk of assassination." She crossed her arms and stared at me as if she'd like to take a bite out of me.

Which isn't a bad idea.

I was surprised. My beast-self, my jaguar, rarely voiced things in words. He communicated more often with a random thought or a picture that flashed through my brain. Not that he wasn't smart. However this part of me perceived the world in a more animalistic, and instinct-driven frame of mind.

Down, boy, I thought, though I knew damned well it wouldn't listen to my more human self. It never did.

I could almost hear a derogatory chuff, but I didn't have time for jaguar games.

"How soon before we meet our pickup?" I said.

"Thirty minutes, boss. At least we're on schedule."

That didn't do us a damn bit of good given we'd muffed the mission.

"Okay, go below deck and find a pair of shorts on this tub."

"Sure, boss," smirked Kane.

"And Gunner, turn your head."

"Why?"

"Just do it."

He turned his head to the sea, and I pounced on our passenger. I yanked the straps of her dress down and fished the phone and jump drives from her bra.

"What the hell?" she yelled. "Get away from me." She squirmed seeking escape, but in a boat bouncing on the surface of the sea, there were few places to go.

"Sorry, ma'am, but you can't keep pieces of evidence."

"Who the fuck are you," she snapped, "to be fishing around in my bra?"

"For today—the United States Government. That's all I can say about the matter."

GUNNER

hen Jeanine screamed, I wanted to grab Ryker and throw the fucker off the boat.

He was our team leader and a damned good one. Ryker saved our raggedy asses more than once, but I disliked him pawing the poor woman who had no choice in traveling with us.

"Hey!" I said.

"Stand down, Gunner," warned Ryker.

One did not mess with the Chief, but the look of shock and fright on our rescue's face clenched my gut. The need to protect her overwhelmed me, and if that meant going against my teammates and closest buddies, I would.

"You know, you could have asked before you manhandled her."

Ryker's eyes flew open at my insubordinate words. *But hell, he was out of line.*

I knelt before Jeanine because I wanted to get eye level with her, and you can't stand on a smallish boat clipping the water at high speed.

"Don't mind him. He's forgotten what women look like."

"Gunner," growled Ryker in warning. But I ignored him.

"What's your name?"

"Jeanine Lee."

"Okay, Jeanine. We will meet up with Coast Guard cutter soon, and it will take us back to the U.S., probably Miami. Is that right, Ryker?"

"Yeah. Miami," Ryker grunted.

"Then you can go where you want."

"Easy for you to say. I've locked my credit cards, ID, and passport in my hotel room in St. Lucia."

"Damon will arrange transportation to your home base. He's our logistics man."

Damon raised his hand. "Here."

"Yeah. We're acquainted. He told me I spoke shitty French."

I glanced at Damon, who, courtesy of his shifter hearing, easily caught her words over the roar of the boat engine. He shrugged his shoulders.

"Mr. Charm has his own way with women," I said.

"All of us do," Kane joked, as he climbed back on deck and handed Ryker his backpack.

"Now," groused Ryker, as he slipped the pack on, "if we'd worked this efficiently on the yacht—"

Damon shifted the boat into a faster gear making us all stumble on the deck. He wasn't in the mood for Ryker's complaints, because we all knew the plan had a high probability of failure. There were too many moving parts and too few of us, and the only one surprised it went into a ditch was our team leader.

We'd put our all into it, but sometimes, despite your best efforts, the op blew apart.

Doesn't mean we won't try again.

Kane's eyes nearly popped when he saw Jeanine's top

pulled down. She wore a bra, but it was a very sexy black lace, and the way Jeanine glared was hot too.

And I liked her much better as a brunette.

"Here," he said, offering another backpack to her. "We have extra clothes in there. Cover your body."

"Why?" she snapped.

"Because we are near the equator and your fair skin will burn redder than a boiled lobster by the time we meet the cutter."

"Oh," she said. Her indignation deflated, and her shoulders drooped. She had been up all night, and her drawn eyes revealed her exhaustion. The morning sun glittered in her tired eyes as dawn broke on the ocean.

"Do we have food?" I asked.

"Here," Ryker responded, pulling out a package of beef jerky from his backpack. He held it out to me.

"Not me. Her. And water too."

And that wasn't a smart move on my part because Ryker's eyes glowed before he offered her the jerky and the water. My jaguar growled inside me disliking the predator's gaze Ryker gave her.

Mine, said my beast.

For the record, I was not a one-woman man. As jaguar shifters, our beasts were normally solitary creatures. We took our pleasures as they came, and I had no problem with that. Traveling the world like we did from one dangerous assignment to another didn't leave lots of room or time for a committed relationship.

But the woman ticked all my boxes. She was spunky, adventurous, fit, and smart. It took a special woman to keep up with me since jaguar shifters were energetic creatures.

Jeanine shivered, so I took the backpack and fished out a gray hoodie. It was a shame to cover her sexy dress, but I hated to see her in distress.

"Here you go."

She pulled it from my hand and slipped it on. I watched her every move. Her fingers and wrists bent in the most graceful way I'd ever seen, and I was fascinated. She'd painted her nails in sparkly gold to match her dress.

"Gunner," snapped Kane standing behind me. "Find something else to do besides staring."

My jaguar growled within me again, and I whipped around to face Kane. I stepped toe-to-toe to him, using my natural feline sense of balance to keep me upright.

"Mind your own business, Doc."

"Maybe it is my business."

"Knock it off you two," said Ryker with his voice low. "Sit down, shut—"

But the boat engine stuttered, and the vessel jolted us with a lurch and then stilled in the water.

"What the hell. Damon?" said Ryker. "What happened?"

"Don't know."

"I'm on it," said Kane. "Raise the engine hatch."

Damon hit the switch to lift the engine hatch at the stern, and the back seat rose to reveal the engine.

"Yep," I said. "It's an engine."

"Smart ass," muttered Kane.

"What do you think you'll do?" said Jeanine. "We're in the middle of the ocean."

"Astute observation. Check the fuel line, the spark plugs, see if I can find a simple fix."

"We call him Doc," I said, "and not just because he's our medic."

"Yeah," said Kane wriggling his hands with a smile. "I'm the man with the hands."

"Stop jawing and get going," said Ryker. "We need to make tracks."

"Can't you just call the cutter to retrieve us?"

"Sure," said Ryker. "If we want to give Morgan a clue where we are. Why do you think he's such a successful pirate? He has a bunch of ships in these waters searching for easy pickings. They are listening for SOSs, sat phone GPS signals, anything that will give them the ship's location."

Her eyes widened, but she asked a question I did not expect.

"How many ships?"

"Three, we think?"

"Have you been watching them for long?"

"What the hell? What's with the questions? And why were you in Morgan's cabin anyway going through his desk? Who the hell are you?"

"No one," she mumbled. Jeanine put on the hoodie as she stared out over the water. And her scent shifted too, with a subtle note of fear, like she's lying.

Ryker's eyes narrowed with suspicion too.

"Gunner," said Kane. "Make yourself useful and find me some tools. They stowed none by the engine."

I looked in the storage sections under the seats, and Damon went below deck to the tiny sleeping space.

"Nothing there," said Damon.

"I've got nothing," I said. There was a length of rope, a blanket, a flare gun, and a first aid kit, and a bottle of whiskey. But no tools.

"Oh for heaven's sake," huffed Jeanine. She fished in her bra and pulled out a metal nail file. "Try this."

Kane smiled with appreciation as he took the thin piece of metal. "A gal after my heart. You know how to improvise, don't you?"

She crossed her arms and settled back in her seat.

"Anything to get us moving," she said.

"Shut your mouth and work," said Ryker. "And you, Gunner, survey the resources."

"Done." I reported the list of what I found and Ryker's expression turned sour.

"Doc, get on that engine."

"For heaven's sake," said Jeanine. "Are you always this grumpy?"

I had to turn away, so he didn't see me laughing. Chief's bad moods when an op didn't go as planned were legendary.

"Chief," said Damon, "is always this grumpy."

"Damon, give Doc a hand," growled Ryker. "We can't sit out here without power."

"Aye, aye, Chief."

"What are you guys anyway?" Jeanine said.

"That's on a need-to-know basis," grumbled Ryker.

"Since I'm on a ship in the middle of the Caribbean with four strangers, I need to know."

Ryker raised an eyebrow and turned away.

"I'll check things down below," he said.

The Chief could be a dick, but it didn't bother us because we gave it right back. But we couldn't in front of the civilian. Her adorable face was now marred by a frustrated frown. So I sat next to her.

"Don't mind him. We let Morgan escape off that ship. It upsets him when an op gets blown."

"Let me get this straight. A mysterious U.S. government four-man team was on a ship of a suspected pirate to kill him? And screwed the op?"

"What were you doing on there? And don't tell me 'to party' because you enter a pirate's private room for only two reasons—to have sex with him, or to steal from him. Which was it?"

"I've got nothing to hide," she said lifting her chin. "A friend of mine partied with Morgan and then disappeared. She sent me a message saying she was in trouble, and then her messages stopped."

"Did you contact the authorities?"

"Which authorities would that be? Who takes an interest in a girl who parties with a suspected criminal?"

I had to admit she a point.

"What's her name?"

"Surma Jones. Black girl, 5'8", about one-hundred-fifty pounds."

"We've been on Morgan's ship for three months. I didn't see her."

She bit her lip, which my inner beast found adorable. He growled within me to get closer, and though in the back of my head I realized I shouldn't, I put my arm around her. Her hair's scent, laden with the sea, and the essence of her wafted up my nose. It was enticing and intoxicating.

Mine, said my jaguar.

Yeah, sure, buddy. And what would we do with her?

Do I have to spell it out?

The urge to nuzzle her neck came over me, and I stopped short of leaning over to put my mouth on her creamy skin. Inside my beastly side complained loudly.

Work, not play.

It was weird scolding yourself, and things got more ridiculous when my manhood stirred. But me making a play for her in front of the team wouldn't work, especially since we were dead in the water and miles from rescue.

"What are you doing there, Gunner?"

Damon looked over his shoulder, and his eyes narrowed. He appeared ticked off.

"I'm being nice."

Jeanine huffed, and I watched her nostrils flare with an unaccustomed level of interest.

"Be nice to her and leave her alone," said Damon.

"Stop your jawing, both of you." Gunner poked an oil-streaked face from the engine compartment. "I don't know. It could be a clogged fuel line. Do we have any wire?"

"There's the snare wire in the survival kit," I said.

"No," he said. "It's too thin. But, damn it, get that kit."

Jeanine huffed. "Do I have to give you every tool?" She fiddled with the clasp of her bra and pulled it through the sleeve of her hoodie. How do women do that? But I didn't understand until she pulled at the stitches of her bra and pulled out an underwire.

"There," she said holding out the curved wire. "If that doesn't work, I'll have destroyed a hundred-dollar bra for nothing."

KANE

Jeanine was smart and resourceful. One thing SEALS admire is a person who can pull solutions from nothing. I didn't know if Jeanine's bra part would work, but I reached out and plucked the curved wire from her hand. Our fingers touched, and a spark of electricity shocked me. Her gorgeous blue eyes widened on contact.

Over her shoulder, dark clouds shadowed the water, and a sense of danger prickled through my body. It would be a disaster to get caught in a storm in a boat like this. The rough waves slapped against the hull of the boat and confirmed my suspicion that we were in for rough weather.

"I don't suppose you have a wrench," I said.

"Here," said Gunner who reached for his backpack. He pulled out a multi-tool with many tools including a saw. It was obviously expensive and not standard issue.

"Geez, you should have given this to me first thing, Gunner."

"Am I the only one that packed their survival kit?"

"No. But you are the only one who didn't use it," I said.

"When you're good—"

"Stow it," I said. "You picked off our kits and left yours alone."

"I gave you my multi-tool."

The SEAL survival kit is a thing of beauty when it's fully packed. It has a slew of useful items from pain relievers to bouillon cubes. But we've been on one mission after another with hardly any time to re-provision. My last government issue multi-tool got lost on the previous mission. And this one that Gunner put in his case was not standard issue. He'd put some dollars into it.

"Thanks. I'll consider it my birthday present."

"Hey!" complained Gunner.

"Stow it," said Damon. "When Ryker pokes his head up here, he'll expect something done."

With a few hard yanks, I disconnected the fuel line, and the few drops you'd expect from the connector didn't spurt from the hose. With the flathead screwdriver of the multi-tool, I dislodged the connector from the fuel line. But instead of diesel, white goo spilled out

"What the hell is that?" said Damon.

"Big problems. Someone put in a product to dry the water in the tank, and it solidified and clogged the fuel line. Nasty business."

"Can you unclog it?"

"Sure, for now. It hasn't clogged up the fuel pump. But I can't guarantee the fuel line won't clog again." I looked at the skyline again, and Damon followed my line of sight.

"I'll go talk to Ryker," Damon said. "We need a Plan B."

"You got one?" Gunner asked.

"Look." Damon pointed to the storm. "There is a small island there. We should make for it."

I peered and barely made out a black dot under the clouds.

"Into the storm?" I said. Gunner appeared as skeptical as I felt.

"Do you want to ride out the storm in this boat?" Damon asked pointedly.

I shook my head and so did Gunner though he crossed his arms over his chest.

"What's going on?" said Jeanine.

No point in sugar coating the obvious. "A storm is coming, and I'm not confident that when I get the fuel restored that the fuel line won't clog again. Damon thinks we should seek refuge on the closest island and wait things out."

"I got that part," she said with sass. "But how will that help us get us to meet that ship?"

Gunner put his arm around her shoulders, but she shrugged it off.

"It's not," I said. "It will keep us alive, which is job one. We'll work out the rest later."

"Great. Wonderful," she said sarcastically. "I'm on a stalled boat in the middle of the ocean with four gung-ho assassins who can't get their shit together. I should have taken my chances with Morgan."

"Don't say that," said Gunner. What was wrong with him? He was hanging all over her, and I'd never seen him pay so much attention to one woman, never mind putting up with this much crap.

"Gunner, give me a hand."

"Sure, Doc."

He knelt next to me.

"What the fuck do you think you're doing?" I snapped at him.

"What?"

"You and the girl."

"Back off, Doc. It's none of your business."

Was it? I didn't like how close he was sitting next to her or the attention he showed her.

"We rescued her. You can refrain from making moves on her."

"What is your problem?"

"Guys," said Ryker as he rose from below decks. Damon came up behind him. "With the threatening bad weather, we need to take cover. How's that engine coming?"

"Clogged fuel line," he grunted. "I'm cleaning it now."

With a quick questioning glance toward Gunner, who stood too closely to Jeanine, I took the fuel line and scooped out the goo with the underwire. Why should I care if Gunner made a play for Jeanine?

Mine.

A heat filled me, and my pants got tighter. I couldn't believe my beast was starting this now, in the middle of the ocean. An enticing scent that wafted from the wire tickled my nose. Jeanine.

Mine, my beast insisted again. I did not have time for this. My team counted on me to get this engine going. The dark clouds rolled faster toward us, and a brisk wind whipped up over the water and rippled the shirts on our bodies. I didn't have time to pay attention to my beast. I'd pay for it later; my jaguar disliked being ignored, but survival was job one.

"Pump the fuel line bulb, Damon," I said.

"What about Gunner?" he said.

"He's busy being nice," I replied snarkily.

"Someone needs to take care of our passenger," said Gunner.

Jeanine rolled her eyes.

"Only because you kidnapped me and put me on this boat. I was doing fine before someone slung me over his shoulder like a caveman."

"Ma'am," said Ryker in his deep rolling voice, "as soon as

we can, we'll get you back to the United States. Until then, just sit back."

"Yeah," said Gunner with a grin, "and enjoy the ride."

Jeanine gave him an incredulous glance for which I did not blame her. I knew these men and put my life in their hands every day. But she didn't.

"Kane," rumbled Ryker. "Tick, tock."

How can this one woman distract me this much?

"Aye, aye, Chief," I said.

"And Gunner, pack up the resources and get our back-packs in one location. We may need to bug out soon."

"Aye, aye, Chief," Gunner echoed.

With Damon's help, I finished cleaning that part of the fuel line. Then clean diesel pumped out of the hose and splashed on my clothes.

"Okay, Damon, stop pumping the bulb now."

"Yeah, right," he grunted oddly, and I twisted my head to see of all damned things, the outline of his cock straining against his pants. What the fuck?

"Holster your weapon, Darkman," I said in a low voice.

"It's my jaguar. He's got a wild hair going."

"Seems to be going around," I replied. I flicked my gaze to Ryker who sat, at least in my estimation, too close to Jeanine.

"Yeah," grumbled Damon.

I reinstalled the connector giving good twists to the nut that held the hose clamp. I glanced up at the sky, but in the downward sweep of my eyes, I caught Jeanine staring at me in fascination. The intensity of her gaze caused my heart to pound as driving electricity pulsed through my blood. If I couldn't touch her, I might go insane. But, the job comes first, not some hair-brained, or rather beast-driven lustful thoughts.

Bending my head to my work, I snapped the connector back into the fuel line assembly.

"Okay, Damon. Crank her up again."

"Again?" he croaked.

Darkman is as stoic as the rest of us. Living and working with a guy for twenty-four-seven you get to know him, and I could tell he was struggling with his cat's attraction to Jeanine, just like me. Ryker looked grumpier than usual, and Gunner kept throwing glances to those two. We were all on edge, and not just from a mission that went sideways.

A crack of thunder rolled over the seas. We'd officially run out of time and had to concentrate on the mission.

"Dude," I said in a low voice. "Keep it freaking together."

"I know, man. I do. This has never happened to me."

"Yeah," I grunted. I was running baseball stats in my head, but my inner jaguar wanted to get near Jeanine and keeping him down was an exercise in extreme self-control. You would think that a Navy SEAL would have that down, but this pull was strong. My hands shook as I pumped the primer valve to get diesel to the engine.

"Start the engine and pray to the jaguar gods that it starts."

Damon took the step across the deck as thunder boomed over the waves, and raindrops hit my face. The boat's rocking grew more intense as the wind picked up. Waves hit with rounding slaps of water. Out on the water things could turn dangerous fast, and this boat was not one to weather a big blow.

"Gunner," said Ryker. "Get a lifejacket on her and take her down below. Damon, turn over that engine!"

"Sure thing, Chief."

Damon engaged the ignition, and the engine chugged and whined, and my heart sank. If that goo reached into the engine, it would kill it. Our only hope was if the engine started.

"Is that pump primed?" yelled Damon over the rushing wind.

I pressed the primer bulb, and it was as hard as a rock.

Like me.

Fuck. I was at full mast as Gunner helped her with a life-jacket and then escorted her down the steps. Her sexy long legs extending from that short dress commanded my attention as she walked.

"Kane!" yelled Damon. Oh hell, I hadn't answered him.

"Yeah!" I said. "It's hard."

"Goddamn it," Damon grunted, and I didn't know whether it was from not getting the engine started or his physical condition which mirrored my own.

"Crank it," I yelled.

"Fuck you," he muttered and pressed the ignition again. The engine sputtered and finally caught.

"Thank god!" he said. Damon throttled the engine higher and turned into the storm toward the island. This was normally bad practice, but it was never good to get caught on the water in a storm like this.

I pulled down the seating of the boat to close off the engine and lurched across the deck to Damon.

"Careful," I yelled in his ear over the engine. "I'm not sure if the engine got any of the goop. If you rev it too high, it could stall."

"We need speed."

"We need to get there."

Damon huffed and peered into the storm-cloud darkened path.

"I'll get us there."

Damon was one stubborn son-a-bitch, something we all appreciated at times. We were trained to get ourselves out of any situation, but Damon did it from sheer strength of will. Which was an advantage to our team, but I was not so sure how it would work with Jeanine? I had to tell him the truth because the last thing I wanted was trouble with my crew.

"Dude," I yelled, "my jaguar says Jeanine is my mate."

Damon made a derisive sound and opened his mouth, but just then a streak of lightning flashed a bright ribbon and thunder cracked in a deafening boom. Electricity cracked in the air, and the sky opened on us as if it wanted to blot us from the face of the churning ocean.

Fuck.

DAMON

ell, no. Jeanine is not Kane's mate. She's mine. I'd never experienced such a powerful reaction to a woman. This emotion came straight from my jaguar, and I could do nothing about it. She was mine, I would convince her of that fact, and these other fuckers will stay away from her, or I would do them serious damage. If we weren't in a life-threatening situation, I'd claim her now. I didn't like that Ryker was in the hold with her. It's tiny and intimate and who knew what ideas he had. I would set them all straight, just as soon as I got us out of this mess. As I opened my mouth to tell Kane this, the air split with light and sound, and it made the beast inside me growl.

As much I tried to heed Kane's warning, I had to push the engines because otherwise, I couldn't make traction against these waves. My jaguar, my intuitive sense, told me this was a bad idea to challenge this brutal weather but I had to go with my head on this. We needed to make landfall. None of us could survive if this boat capsized. As SEALs, we were all strong swimmers, and as jaguars, stronger, but few people, human or shifter could survive in a storm-tossed ocean. And

Jeanine? Her chances were virtually nil, and I couldn't let her come to harm.

Ryker climbed onto the deck.

"I'll take the wheel," he said. "Get in that hold."

"I'm good," I said.

"I know it," he replied. "But I have to protect my shadow."

A group of jaguars was called a shadow, which was why we called ourselves Team Shadow. That name graced the identifying patches of our uniforms. Other SEALs thought it meant we were advertising our stealth, but we called ourselves what we were—a team of jaguar shifters, put together by top brass five years ago.

"Okay, Chief," I said giving him the wheel. I nodded my head to Gunner and Kane, and Kane went first, then Gunner tossed the backpacks down. After him, I headed into the tiny hold that barely fit all of us.

Jeanine sat on the deck with her knees drawn up and her hands clasped around them. She stared at all of us with her bright blue eyes that made my heart pound. Her too rapid breathing told me that she was excited or frightened, and my jaguar, damn him, didn't care which.

"What's going on, guys?" she said. Jeanine chewed on her lip, and her eyes darted to each of us.

"That's on a need-to-know basis," Gunner quipped, who hadn't met a bad joke he didn't like. Couldn't he sense her terror?

"We're taking cover," I said. Ryker is piloting the boat."

"Will we be okay?"

"Sure," said Kane as he sank to sit next to her. "We trust Ryker with our lives. He'll pull us through."

"Ryker's the one who freed this boat out from the sinking yacht," she said as if she were sleepwalking. I worried that she was going into shock. She was not a soldier and didn't have our intense training.

Gunner sank next to her, the fucker, and put an arm around her.

"It will be fine. We've been in worse scrapes."

Sometimes Gunner's ability to gloss over the seriousness of a situation was an asset. However, a strange look flickered in Jeanine's eyes that told me she didn't believe Gunner. I didn't blame her. The boat rocked fiercely, and I didn't feel the forward motion I should when the engines propelled a boat forward in the water. The boat could stall any minute. She was smart and figured out we were in big trouble.

Kane sat next to her on her left, and I knelt before her and took her hands clasped on her knees.

"We will get you through this safely," I said. "I promise you that."

"So do I," said Gunner.

"Yes," said Kane in a husky voice. His eyes were slits which signaled to me he wasn't thinking about the danger we were in.

No. He contemplated another form of danger—that of touching my mate.

Either it was her fear or her pheromones that filled the hold, but my jaguar wasn't particular. Her scent intoxicated me, and judging by Kane and Gunner's blown pupils, they felt that way too.

My jaguar was ready to take her. The urge to mate strikes lightning fast, and before this day I had no reason to deny it. I had no problem attracting women when I wanted. That was a gift from my jaguar side that exuded an animal magnetism that women found hard to resist.

The engine sputtered and stilled, and the boat rocked harder.

Ryker entered the hold in one jump and pulled the hatch tight with a bang.

"I hope that's a goddamn watertight seal," he snapped angrily.

When he turned to face us, his eyes narrowed.

"What the hell is happening?" he said.

"You tell me," Jeanine said. Her eyes begged for a good word on our situation, but that was not happening.

"That boat stalled and we're in the middle of a storm, and we didn't get close enough to the island to swim for it."

"Swim?" she squeaked.

"Can you?" he growled.

"Yes, but not in weather like this."

"Ryker, give her a break," said Kane. "She's a civilian."

"I'm perfectly aware of the situation," he said. Ryker's frustration came through in his voice, and I understood. Our mission had gone to crap, and so had our exit. We were miles from the Coast Guard boat that was supposed to pick us up, and we all knew in weather like this, their first responsibility was to respond to distress calls. The oceans were heavily trafficked, and most could not avoid the weather.

"I told her we'll make sure she's safe."

"We will," he said. "We can't help it, can we?"

He flicked a glance to each of us, and in this little, dimly lit cabin in a storm-tossed and disabled powerboat, I understood what he meant.

Ryker was no fool. He watched all of us like a hawk. Aside from the fact that losing a team member lessened all of our chances for survival, he protected us with his sure Alpha sense of right and wrong. He wouldn't let us hurt each other over a woman.

Kane pursed his lips and found something interesting to inspect on the bulkhead. Gunner stared with a challenge to Ryker, but he had it all wrong. Ryker's Alpha scent released as it would in stressful conditions. He was dominating us, and we'd submit to his will, but it ticked something in Jeanine's head too, because her pupils had grown wide.

"What's happening?" said Jeanine.

"Nothing," said Ryker. "We're riding out this storm and hoping we don't capsize."

"Sure," snorted Kane. "Sugarcoat it for the lady."

"What happens if we capsize?" Her voice trembled.

"Things get a little difficult," said the overly optimistic Gunner.

"I'm hoping this storm blows over fast," Ryker said, "and Gunner can get the engine started again. Don't worry. The situation is serious, but we've been in far worse scrapes."

She shook her head as if fighting something off. "So I've heard," she said derisively. Jeanine appeared not to bend to Ryker's chemical persuasion. Was it because she wasn't a shifter?

The boat rocked, but no thunder sounded, and the rain eased. This was not the good news it appeared, and a glance to my teammates confirmed it. Only a big storm would have an eye where the weather calmed.

"Maybe it's passing," said Jeanine hopefully.

"Most likely we are in the storm's eye," said Kane grimly. "When it passes over us it will hit hard again."

"Hey," said Gunner. He reached his hand to the bulkhead at his side. "There's an inflatable here."

"Good," Ryker said. "We may have to use it."

"Inflatable?" said Jeanine.

"Either boat or raft. If the ship goes down, we'll have something to hang onto."

"Aren't you worried about sharks?" she said.

Gunner laughed. "They worry about us."

She bit her lip again, and my eyes couldn't help but concentrate on her full lips. My teammates did the same thing. Jeanine's eyes morphed into giant pools of anxiousness as she glanced at each of us, who eyed her intently.

"What's going on guys?"

Gunner's eyes glowed green like they do when he's about to shift, and the musk in the tiny space grew thick.

"What?" she squeaked.

"Chill, Gunner," ordered Ryker.

"Not sure I can, boss," Gunner said.

"We're all having that problem," grumbled Kane.

"Yes," said Ryker, "we are."

"I don't understand," said Jeanine.

"You don't have to worry," said Ryker. "None of us could do anything you don't want. Can we?"

"Nope," said Kane.

"No," I replied.

"Gunner?" rumbled Ryker.

"Nah."

Kane bent his head and nuzzled her neck. She turned to meet his eyes with hers, wide in surprise.

"Are you purring??"

"Guess so, doll," he said. And as he said it, the rumbles from deep within each of us grew more audible.

"Wait," she exclaimed, "you're all purring! What the hell?!"

"Don't you like it, baby?" said Gunner. He kissed the top of her head, and I tell you it was an exercise in self-control not to tear him or Kane off of her. I moved forward, and Ryker put his hand on my shoulder.

"Big cats in the wild purr to calm their prey," declared Jeanine. Her gaze swept the hold as she regarded each of us. I sensed her nervousness and heard the uptick of her heart.

"Stand down," Ryker ordered.

"But—" It was not like me to disobey, but Jeanine upended my world. These weren't my teammates but competitors for the same female. Even my Alpha's orders weren't enough to stay the beast within.

"Guys, I get it," said Jeanine. "It's a good joke, but you can stop now. I get it. You're pranking me, probably trying to take my mind off the seriousness of our situation. But this is getting scary now, so please stop."

"We're not trying to scare you," I said.

"And we're not pranking you," said Gunner.

Ryker glanced at his watch and knelt, knowing an eye of a storm passes in ten to thirty minutes.

"There's a lot to explain, Jeanine. I doubt these chowderheads get it either. And we barely know you. But you present an unusual situation."

"Me? Let's see," said Jeanine. "You kidnapped me from a pirate's yacht, the engine of our getaway vehicle failed, and you are all acting strange. Oh, and all of you purr. And you say this I'm unusual? Gee. I don't know what you're talking about. Just another normal day for me. Seems like I'm the least unusual person here."

Gunner chuckled. "I like your sense of humor."

"You think I'm amused?" she said. Her tone challenged Gunner, but little did she know that Gunner didn't mind a sassy woman.

Neither did I.

"I'm not laughing," she said. "I want out of this boat and to get back to St. Lucia where I have a nice hotel room waiting."

"No," said Ryker. "We can't let you go there. That's Morgan's last known location. He'll kill you."

"You are not my boss," she said.

"No," he said. "I'm not. Something else."

"That's it," she said, pushing to her feet. "This is creepy. I'd rather be in the ocean than spend another minute with you guys."

In a flash, she sprinted toward the hatch and climbed the

ladder and tried to undo the latch, but Ryker put his arms around her waist and swung her around.

"You don't want to go topside. There are hundreds of miles of ocean around us, and you won't survive."

"What will I do here, with four men who look at me like I'm lunch?"

"Oh, no," said Ryker huskily. "Not lunch." He bent his head and kissed her.

I watched, and my jaguar growled instinctually, without my permission. Ryker broke the kiss, and his eyes met mine.

"Get up there with Kane and start the engine. We'll need it to weather this storm."

*D*amon and Kane filed past us, as grim as could be, imparting sideways glances at both of us. Their furtive expressions gave me the impression Ryker tossed them from a party they wanted to attend.

"Get moving," reiterated Ryker.

"What about Gunner?"

"Me?" said Gunner. "I'm surveying the supplies down here."

"Yeah, yeah," said Kane derisively.

Rain pelted in, slicking the deck with water before Damon and Kane shut the hatch on us.

"Will they be okay?" I asked.

"We train for this," said Ryker. "Are you okay?"

"I'm scared shitless," I admitted.

"Let me reassure you," said Ryker.

Ryker's mouth possessed mine. He held me tight to him, so there was no doubt in my mind what he wanted. His tongue swept into my mouth, my flesh met his in an addictive dance that spread tingles through me. This churn of pleasure felt just too damn good to stop. His hard muscles were damn sexy, and his alluring scent made me lightheaded; my knees wobbled. Where's my head at though? This must be the world's worst timing because I shouldn't be kissing anyone while the boat swirled in a deadly combination of calm and destruction. You could call it madness, but my body responded to him like we were a matched pair, not strangers who'd just met. All sense of logic completely brushed aside, I responded in kind, hungrily devouring his kisses with ones of my own.

And I was aware of Gunner watching us intently, and this was exciting too. Who knew I had an exhibitionist streak?

Ryker slid his hand under the hem of my dress and caressed my inner thighs causing me to shiver. I liked this far too much in my present circumstances, and if I could think straight, I would tell myself this was insane. But my thoughts firmly centered on how good it felt to have him stroke my inner thighs, and inch higher. His fingertips quested inside my panties.

Gunner nibbled the back of my neck, startling me, but the surprise immediately turned into a whimper.

"Sweetheart," said Gunner in a husky voice. "I can't keep my hands off of you." One reached around and cupped my breast.

Ryker gripped my waist and pulled my body into his. "You know what this means, Gunner. All or none."

Gunner growled behind my ear which sent shivers down my spine.

"Yeah," Gunner said. His voice rumbled with want which drew a meow from my throat.

Gunner squeezed my bottom. I never imagined I would like having two men touch me at once, but everything about this day has been strange. One part of me knew that I should step back from them but the other part, told me strangely that I was safe with them; that it was only natural to give in to my desire.

Ryker slipped his fingers inside my panties, and Gunner sensuously drew off my hoodie while nibbling my neck. My knees grew weak, and I melted against Ryker as Gunner pulled the straps of my dress down my arm then licked my spine with his tongue. It was too much and not enough. My breath hitched, and my head spun on this sexual high. I was ready to do anything these two gorgeous men wanted me to do.

Gunner peppered my neck with lingering kisses while Ryker's questing fingers parted my folds slick with my juices. Heat spread through my body as he located my hardened nub that pulsed with the rhythm of my stuttering heart. His thumb stroked it gently, and I rocked against his hand. The tips of his index and middle fingers rested at my entrance as if waiting for my permission.

"Ryker," I gasped.

"You ok doll?" His voice was a low rattle that picked at my fevered emotions like a guitarist playing his instrument.

"Yes, don't stop," I barely managed to whisper because I was beyond sense and plunging into a well of pure sensation.

Ryker's fingers found my core and pushed his fingers into me.

Gunner pressed his hips into my ass so that I could feel his hard length between my cheeks. His fingers played with my nipples twisting and pinching, and I couldn't help but moan.

Ryker found my g-spot and my heart raced as he stroked me with his unrelenting digits. I jutted my hips against his hand taking those marvelous fingers as deep inside as they'd go. I was on fire, and my breathing drew in ragged breaths, and my mind burned with want and need. My core was a flame, and Ryker stoked the fire with his fingers, murmuring how amazing I was.

"You're so beautiful, baby," he said. "I love your body and your hot, tight pussy."

His dirty talk sent me over the edge. My stomach tightened, and I tossed my head reflexively as I exploded in a rush of white heat. Ryker's fingers quested deeper inside me, as I pulsed around them.

"That's it, baby," said Gunner as he pressed my nipples between his fingers. The tugging from my body against his hands gave me one aftershock after another.

I was still aflame. Though I came once, I wanted more. Gunner understood because he let go off my breasts and slid to his knees. While Ryker held me, Gunner buried his face between my legs and lapped at my wet cream and swollen lips, finding me enervated. The tip of his tongue tickled it, and I gasped. His mouth and his tongue lapped my clit and my folds, and I moaned shamelessly. Other men may have kissed me intimately, but none did it with the reckless abandon of Gunner who, judging by his own moans, enjoyed what he was doing thoroughly. Then he speared me with his marvelous tongue, and it entered me just as Ryker's fingers had, and I couldn't help it. I exploded again, this time screaming.

"Gunner!"

My world tilted off its axis. I had no control over this and wanted none. These men wanted me and, damn it, I wanted them too.

Breathing hard, I leaned into Ryker, because my body was now putty. One man, or two, I wanted this and more. Their two sexy scents engulfed me, and I quivered at every lick and stroke to my body. It wasn't just how hot they both were, even though they were smoldering, but they touched with such reverent desire, I could feel the emotion coursing through. I hadn't ever been touched like this before. I'd found heaven, and I wasn't ready to relinquish it.

Ryker kissed me passionately while Gunner stood and wrapped his hands around my waist. He put his mouth on my shoulder, and his teeth dug into my skin.

"Not yet," said Ryker in a warning tone.

Gunner cursed, but pulled away, sputtering something under his breath that I couldn't hear.

"What's wrong?" I said.

But the hatch flew open, and a sudden rush of wind swallowed my words. The boat lurched sending Ryker and me against one bulkhead and Gunner against the other.

"Fuck," said Gunner.

"Gunner, get the lifejackets, and that rope behind you."

Gunner looked over his shoulder. "Oh, yeah."

Ryker slipped the lifejacket Gunner handed him on me and checked the buckles. "Safety, first," he said as he snapped the buckles closed.

He and Gunner both donned lifejackets, and then he took two others Gunner handed him.

"If the boat rocks too much grab the inflatable and both of you get on deck."

"Aye, Chief," said Gunner.

Ryker climbed the stairs and shut the hatch, and I turned to face Gunner who smiled at me.

"We're in big trouble, aren't we?" I said.

He shrugged. "Define trouble."

My journalist's Spidey senses told me we were in deep shit. The rain fell like a waterfall on the deck above in a continuous curtain of white noise. I couldn't hear the guys speaking above, and the engine still hadn't started.

"We're all screwed, and we will die."

"We will not," Gunner said. "But the screwing part? That's something I'd like to work on."

He delivered his crude words with a smile and such charm they were a compliment, and my fraught core warmed at them. But was this inappropriate? The pause in our completely illogical amorous adventure gave me time to question what the hell was happening to me. It was like I'd been possessed by some kind of animalistic desire that had shut down all rational thought.

I could tell from Gunner's face how much danger we were in. The boat bucked under my seat, and I scrambled for the wooden ledge that served as a seat in the small hold of this vessel. My fingers dug into the underside of the ledge, trying to keep myself upright as the boat pitched and rose at a steep angle in the churning water.

"What's going to happen?" I squeaked.

"It depends on how rough the water is. Ryker right now is tying up breakaway harnesses from the rope for us and then tying up the inflatable. If the swells get too high, they could capsize us. Then he'll have us go up top and put us in a harness, and we'll ride it out there. It will be wet, but safer than being down below if the boat capsizes. Don't worry. We'll protect you."

"You make this sound like it's not a big deal. But it is."

"We go into dangerous situations at least once a week and can't afford to let the danger affect our thinking. We were trained and still train hard to come out of the impossible alive. Each of us knows what to do to keep kicking."

"Except me."

"Yeah, but we'll protect you."

"What did Ryker mean, 'not yet?'"

Gunner's face in the dim light flushed. "He's protecting you, is all."

"No," I said with heat. These evasive answers did not cut it for me. "That's not what he meant."

"If—no—when, we get out of this, we'll all be having a talk

with you and we'll explain it then. Right now survival is job one."

"I thought this wasn't a big deal for you," I replied.

"Doesn't mean it's not a job," he snapped.

So I *could* get a rise out the unflappable Gunner. He cared about his work and took pride in it. That's not such a bad quality for a man to have. Still, he ticked me off, and it probably showed in my face.

"Sorry," he said. "This is an unusual situation for me, I mean, us."

"And since I know you're not talking about us being stranded on a boat in the middle of a storm, it would help me if you didn't keep in the dark."

Without warning, thunder pealed around us, and caught me off-guard. I shrieked. Gunner plopped next to me and put his strong arm around my shoulder.

"It's okay. It's just thunder."

"I know," I said. Damn. Some days the bravado of being a kick-ass newspaper woman wore too thin. What I wanted to do, was bury my face in Gunner's chest and let him hold me tight and safe against danger.

The rumble of the ship's engines greeted my ears, and I sighed with relief. At least one thing had gone right, right?

But the hatch popped open, and Ryker's face hung there with a face so serious you would think we sat at a funeral.

"You two better get up here now."

RYKER

The powerboat tossed on the waves, swirling to twist the boat. If we couldn't turn the vessel into the waves, one could wash over us and capsize us. I'd stared into danger and death more times that I could count, but nothing made my heart beat so hard as to think my mate might die under my watch.

Mate.

Sometimes the jaguar side of me played really well with the human part, and we were an effective team. But he was a wild creature, my jaguar barely under the control of my human half. With the woman who he wanted to claim as our mate under our noses, I could hardly contain him. In the hold with her and Gunner, it was a battle not to let him take control. The animal within me wanted so much more than touching her intimate flesh.

But it wasn't time for play, and I had our asses to save. Grudgingly my wild part gave way to my more sensible side.

Nor would I let any of my team make their play to claim her until she understood fully what she faced. Not just one jaguar shifter, but four wanted her, and I couldn't help but think that would blow any woman's mind.

Speaking of blowing.

Nope. My mind can't go down there. I had to focus on tying these knots for our makeshift harnesses. As I did, I glanced at Damon and Kane fighting wind and rain to start the engine again. I could scarcely hear what they said to each other over wind gusts that tossed us around like a child splashing a rubber ducky in his bath.

"Now!" said Kane, and Damon lurched to the wheel and cranked the engine. It sputtered, and Kane cursed.

"Again!" He buried his fingers deep into the engine's mechanism, and risked his digits, but he understood the danger we faced. If he had to slice off a finger or two, he'd get the engine started.

But then again, with our aberrant shifter DNA, they'd grow back, eventually.

Damon cranked the engine again, and it turned slowly as if the battery was low, and I cursed. We couldn't afford a failed battery—not now.

"Fuck, you piece of shit—start!" Kane spat.

As if inspired by Kane's insult, the engine sputtered on the next crank of the beast. He wriggled his fingers, massaging something in its guts, and it roared to life, finally catching.

I'm not a religious man, but I sent a prayer of thanks to whatever God watched out for us now.

"Turn her into the waves," I called, as if Damon was an idiot who didn't know the proper procedure. He shook his head but didn't complain. We were all on edge about our situation, even if we didn't show it on our faces. Over the years they had learned to take my asshole behavior in stride.

Despite the strong wind, Damon turned her into the swells, and the bow rose as whitecaps crashed against the prow. Rain and spray pelted us as I secured the inflated raft in the middle of the deck with lines running to each of us. I tied Damon's and Kane's harnesses to the metal rails running along the gunwales. My feet slipped on the water-soaked deck as the ship bucked against the rolling water. The weather turned nastier as the waves grew. It wasn't safe for Jeanine to remain below deck.

I yanked open the hatch and called them up. Gunner wisely had Jeanine put on a lifejacket, though I would have taken a piece of his hide if he hadn't. He also dragged up the backpacks. That was the good thing about Gunner. He kept an eye on the details.

The downpour drenched her clothes and slicked her hair, so it dripped water in her eyes. I pushed her onto a seat as I lashed her to the raft with one rope and the gunwale with another. Then I tied the line to the rail with a reef knot, which looked like half a bow.

"If the ship tips over, pull this cord." I had to yell at her above the wailing squall.

She nodded, and I hoped to God she heard me above the wind.

Gunner lashed his own harness and tied himself into my contraption. Now all of us circled the life raft that held our slim hope of survival.

Next Gunner gave me two of our backpacks to tie into the raft, and he secured the other two. Then he lashed himself to the gunwale rails. All we had left to do was stay with the raft, which had the survival supplies.

But we weren't catching any breaks here, and all we could do was hold on as if our lives depended on it, which they did.

I was glad we had a full raft, though individual life rafts would have been better. Those things sealed up around you like a cocoon. And while you'd toss like a bitch inside them, you'd stay safe in almost any blow.

We could only hope that the storm rolled over us and left us in calmer seas, but until then we'd have to ride Neptune's anger out.

Gunner sat next to a shivering Jeanine. We might be in the middle of the Caribbean, but it was a cold deluge that hit us. I sat on her other side and tied my anchor line with another reef knot. Damon sat with grim determination at the wheel, unwilling to let go.

Water drops danced and spun on the deck like crazy ballerinas while the boat's engine chugged against the force of the heaving sea. Even with the wind's whine rushing over us, I heard the small sounds of distress from Jeanine's throat. She'd been a trooper through this, but the overpowering weather and her day so far had to be too much for her. Hell, it was almost too much for me, and I trained and ran ops in waters like these. I put my arm around her to comfort her.

"We will be fine," I said. "You've got the best Navy SEAL team in the world watching out for you."

She stared at me with a defiant expression that told me she didn't believe me.

In considering the events of the day, I had trouble believing it myself.

The boat rocked and spun from an overpowering gust that would have thrown us on the deck or overboard if we hadn't secured our bodies to the vessel. Damon valiantly tried to turn back into the waves, but then a wall of water roared up over us.

I swallowed hard, because though I'm brave, foolhardy, or both, I knew the odds of coming out of this alive.

Damon pushed the engine to the limit, ignoring Kane's earlier warning because we had to get over the crest of that wave before it smashed on us. If we didn't, we'd die.

The tiny boat climbed, its engine strained against the

slope but finally broke the crest, and I breathed with relief because we'd cheated death one more time.

But then another, smaller, but forceful wave crashed over the bow, and swamped us with water. We were going under, no doubt about it.

My team and I locked eyes knowing what would happen next. We all pulled our lash cords, and I pulled Jeanine's freeing us from the gunwales. Another wave poured more water into the boat tossing us into the stormy ocean along with the raft.

My plan was a desperate one, based on our superior strength and swimming skills, but trying to pile into a raft during this blow was dangerous too. We could easily tangle in the lines, get pulled under and drown.

But we'd drown if I hadn't attached us to the raft, so as my foster mother used to say, six and a-half dozen of the other.

The raft slammed in the ocean and bobbed up. I held onto my line and Jeanine's to keep them from getting tangled.

I grabbed her and with the force of my arms tossed her into the bottom of the raft. She flopped on the yellow raft and then turned and spit out a mouthful of water.

"What the hell!" she yelled.

"Hold on to the lines." I yanked at the rope that circled the raft. "Don't let go." And to the rest, I ordered, "Fucking swim," as if it needed explaining. I didn't want us caught in the undertow of the overturned boat going under. It hadn't yet, but all I saw was a thin sliver of bow pointing toward the darkened sky. It was a good thing I pulled Jeanine and Gunner out of the hold when I did, because otherwise, they'd be dining in Davy Jones' locker tonight.

We swam and pulled the raft as it bobbed on the water. Now our goal was different. Instead of trying to head into the waves, we swam with the current, trying to keep on top of the swells. I hoped that as quickly as the bad weather had come upon us, it would depart just as quickly.

My team were strong swimmers, stronger than usual because they were shifters, but as I looked over my shoulder, I could see them tiring. Each of their eyes glowed with a green light that told me they were calling on their beasts for extra strength.

As we strove against the might of the sea, a shaft of yellowish light broke through the dark clouds. The winds eased, the rain turned to a drizzle, and the waves calmed. The storm had passed us, and now we were at the far edge.

"In the raft," I commanded. We all needed a break including me, and I wanted to make sure my - I mean, our mate, wasn't the worse for wear.

One by one we piled in. Gunner pulled a water bladder from one pack and passed it to Jeanine.

"More water?" she said incredulously. "I've seen enough water to last a lifetime."

"Strange as it may seem, you should keep hydrated," he replied. Jeanine took it and winced when she drank the liquid that had sat in the bladder for a couple days. It didn't taste like fresh spring water, but we'd all moved past that during training.

She tried to hand the bladder to Gunner, but he pointed to Damon. Everyone drank, and I assessed our situation. I didn't see land, and I had no idea how far off course we were. We could drift like this for days. Team Shadow could handle it, but Jeanine? I wasn't sure. It's no fun being adrift in the ocean for days on end, so I made an executive decision.

"Hand me the sat phone, Gunner."

"Wait. You have a satellite phone?" said Jeanine in dismay. "Why didn't you use it before?"

"Because anyone can track a sat phone if they're listening and we were trying to get away. But I'm hoping now that

Morgan's associates are too busy with the aftermath of the storm to get to us before we make our escape even if they do notice."

"Here you go, Chief," said Gunner. He tossed the phone at me, and I almost lost it in the water, but caught it at the last second.

"Way to go, Chief," Damon commented.

"But who do you call?" said Jeanine.

"Ghostbusters," smirked Gunner.

"Oh, geez," said Jeanine. "Original, Gunner."

Kane laughed. "She got you, Gun."

"Ha," said Gunner. "No, babe. Ryker will switch on the automatic SOS, and hopefully, that will lead our ride to our location."

"Our ride?"

"And who are you calling 'babe,'" said Damon. He glared at Gunner.

Oh boy. Here we go.

"Stand down, Damon. We've something to discuss."

"What would that be?" Kane rumbled in a low growl.

"Not here. Not now.

"Why the hell not?" Damon questioned.

"Hey, guys…," Jeanine interrupted. "How long will it take for a ship to pick us up?"

GUNNER

*W*as Jeanine trying to deflect the rising tension between us with her question? The ocean slapped the sides of the raft as we stared at each other contemplating the unthinkable. In my mind's eye, I saw my brethren in their animal forms with their ears pinned back and their chatoyant eyes glowing green.

Jeanine stared at us intently, and her hands dug into her thighs as she heard Damon growl.

"Hey," she said too sunnily. "I thought you guys purred instead of growled."

Damon lurched toward Jeanine. His animal's instinct was now in control though he hadn't shifted. Ryker jumped Damon and hauled him backward.

"Stand down."

Damon let loose a loud feral roar as he struggled with our Alpha. Jeanine shrieked and pushed back away from him. Kane joined in, and the two forced Damon on his back.

"Get ahold of yourself, Darkman," said Kane.

Damon stared up into the sky as his breath came out in hard chugs.

"What's wrong with him?"

I scooted to her side and put my arms around her.

"PTSD," I said. "You've heard of it?"

Ryker shot me a warning glance. He was an upfront guy and knowing him like I do, figured he did not like me lying to her. But were we going to expose our true selves to our mate on a raft in the middle of the churning sea?

"I know what it is. Does he always have it this bad?"

"Gunner," warned Ryker.

"Not like this," I blurted. I gave him a hard stare trying to communicate with him that we shouldn't scare Jeanine with the revelations of our true form. Ryker chewed his lip but nodded in understanding.

Damon thrashed and growled, and Jeanine watched him with concern on her face.

"Will he be okay?" said Jeanine.

Damon clutched her leg, but she pulled back.

"Won't someone help him?" Jeanine said. She sat with her back to the wall of the raft, an expression caught between fear and concern on her face. I could tell she wanted to flee. But there was no place to go.

Damon chuffed in deep breaths, and as I leaned forward to remove Damon's hand, Jeanine put hers on mine and shook her head. She stared at Damon as if trying to parse what was happening then slipped to her knees and put her hands on Damon's head.

"Chill, big guy," she said soothingly. "It's okay. We're all here. You'll be fine." We watched in amazement as Damon calmed as she stroked his hair.

This woman had guts to get near a soldier ready to lose his shit. Granted she didn't know he was a shifter, but she had to know that he was dangerous, regardless.

Damon shook his head and then looked into Jeanine's eyes.

"Hey," he said, "what happened?"

Jeanine pulled her hands away.

"Hey, don't stop, doll. That felt good."

"You look better," said Jeanine.

"You flipped out there," said Ryker with a scowl.

"Your PTSD," chimed in Kane.

Damon stared at Kane for a long second until it sunk into his head.

"Yeah, right," he said. "You don't know how to keep your mouth shut, do you, Doc? What about doctor/patient confidentiality?"

"That's for real doctors and real patients," snorted Kane. "Besides, it was Gunner who ratted you out."

"Nothing's sacred." He sat up and looked out over the water and the sinking sun spreading pink on the horizon. "Looks like calm seas tonight."

"How do you get that?" said Jeanine.

"Red in the morning and all," offered Kane.

"Is that true?"

"In middle latitudes, yes," said Kane. "And we are in a middle latitude. Lower latitudes, not so much."

"So what will we do?" asked Jeanine.

"Drift and wait for rescue," said Ryker.

"That doesn't sound like much of a plan."

"If we see an island, we'll make for land," said Damon.

"We've got water for a few days if we're careful, and food," said Ryker.

"And we have each other," said Kane.

Jeanine looked at the water that collected in the raft's bottom. "Is this plastic monstrosity leaking?"

"Nah," I said. "This is usual. Waves splashing over the side —spray."

"Can you get rid of it?"

"Do you see a pail here?"

Jeanine threw her head back to the edge of the raft. "Wonderful. In a wet raft in the open water as night is falling." She shivered.

"You cold, doll?" said Damon.

"Tired," she said.

"Yeah," I said. "It's been a tough day."

"You think?" she said.

"Well, let's do this," said Damon. He slid next to her. "Let's share body heat."

"Damon," growled Kane.

"No, wait," said Ryker. "Kane you take the other side, and, Gunner, get some shut-eye, and I will take the first lookout."

"Hey," I objected.

"Then Damon will take next watch, while you help keep Jeanine warm. Then I'll switch out with Kane. By the time morning comes we'll see where the tide has taken us."

I scooted over to Ryker.

"What are you doing?" I said in a low whisper. Damon and Kane's ears were as good as mine, but they were preoccupied in settling next to Jeanine.

"Look," he said in just as low a tone, "are you not getting it? There are four shifters here who think one woman is their mate. There is only one of two ways this goes down. One— we fight each other to the death. Do you want that?"

"No, of course not."

"So there's door number two. We share."

"What! Are you out of your ever-loving mind?"

"Possibly. But I can't see any other way. It's that, or this unit breaks apart. And if your cat is as insistent as mine, there is no way any of us can walk away from her."

"I hate this idea."

"I'm not fond of it myself. Do you have another option?"

I scratched my day's scruff and couldn't come up with a replacement idea. With my glance at Damon and Kane cradling my mate between them, my jaguar growled within. But Damon, Kane, and Ryker were closer than brothers to me. We'd been through hell and back. You could say that I loved them as brothers, and I wanted them to have every good thing possible.

Jeanine was a good thing. Loving Jeanine was better.

"But isn't it strange," I said to Ryker, "that all four of us see her as our mate?"

"Hell, Gunner, what do we know about how we became what we are?"

"Apparently born that way," I said. "At least that's what the Navy researchers said."

"Yeah. I wondered about that too. They didn't seem especially shocked."

Ryker was right. They weren't. The researchers' treatment of us had been routinely clinical as if they'd done all of the work before.

"Do you think there are others like us?"

"I have seen no SEAL units that match us in strength or agility. But when they had us in research, I heard one of the Navy doctors talk about a group of guys who could be shifters who left the service. No one had seen them since."

"Shifters?"

"Where do you think I got the term?"

Come to think of it, it was Ryker who called us shifters first.

Jeanine's steady breathing told me she'd settled into troubled sleep. Kane and Damon's rumbling purrs indicated they would sleep soon as well. The full moon rose in the sky, shining like a huge white pearl in the darkness.

"I used to study ancient mythology," said Ryker. "Jaguars feature heavily in pre-Colombian lore. There's a region in Colombia, around the town of San Agustin where there are tons of jaguar statues, with faces of men, but large eyes and fangs like cats. What we know of their mythology, is that the central god is a jaguar god. He is the god of fire, who rules the underworld at night and shines his light on the earth during the day. His wife is a jaguar goddess, who rules over midwifery and war."

"So the wife works two jobs, eh?" I said.

Ryker shrugged.

"I guess it keeps her out of trouble," he said with a wry smile.

"There are other depictions of jaguar demi-gods as warriors and protectors. We don't know a lot about their stories, but they were important in different myths. There are plenty of representations of them carved in stone. Maybe they weren't gods, Gunner. Perhaps they were a separate ancient sentient race."

"Come on," I snorted.

"In all the myths of the world, there's always at least one god that's half-beast and half-man. Egypt had Anubis, the jackal-headed god. India has Lord Ganesha, the god with the elephant head. In Mesopotamia, there was Ereshkigal, the winged goddess of the underworld who had taloned feet. Greek gods turned into animals at will, like Zeus, who, if he couldn't seduce a woman with his human form, found an animal form that would do the trick. The list goes on, Gunner. Why would humans associate so many deities with beastly features? I suspect at one time shifters like us could have lived in greater numbers before humans populated every corner of the globe."

"I've never thought about it, Ryker. I found out what I was ten years ago when they brought me to the facility to work with you guys."

"I always thought I was different," said Ryker. "I just didn't know how different. During my teenage years, I had odd blackouts. My foster parents didn't know what to do with me, but then they were going through their own troubles. They had lots of fights, and I'd get restless and slip out of the house to get away from it. They weren't bad people, just too little money and too many kids in the house. I think it relieved them when I asked to get the state's permission to sign up for the Marines at seventeen."

"I didn't have that experience. My adoptive parents were crazy in love and had more than enough to spoil me rotten. It did not thrill them I wanted to sign up for the Navy. But I wasn't that good of a student and couldn't see myself going to college, and I wanted to see the world, so the Navy it was. So you could say that I mostly had a stress-free life until I signed up."

Ryker chuckled.

"So back to the myths," I said. "All the animal-formed gods and goddess live in the underworld?"

"Not all, but it's a theme."

"But they are warriors and protectors?"

"Yes and tied to the medical arts."

He nodded toward our medic Kane who moved to snuggle closer to Jeanine.

"But what's Jeanine's part in all this?" I said. "Why would one woman be the mate for four shifters?"

"I don't know. When we get out of this mess, we should try to find some other shifters."

"Is that the brightest idea? If the government knows about them and hasn't told us, there must be a good reason."

"There you go again, trusting the brass. How many times did I tell you to keep one eye open around those guys?"

"They haven't done wrong by us."

"Not yet," said Ryker. "It's possible they haven't figured out what to do with us. Or they might have other plans that we might not approve."

"One thing that's reliable about you, Ryker, is your healthy sense of paranoia."

"It's kept us alive, hasn't it?"

That's true. Ryker watched our six and kept us out of deep trouble many times.

My eyes strayed to Jeanine again. My breath hitched, and my jaguar stirred within uneasiness, watching my brothers-in-arms spooning her. I wondered just how this could work out without four jaguar shifters killing each other.

KANE

"Hey," said a voice in the dark with a hiss. "Time for your watch."

What the hell? No. I did not want to move from this warm spot with Jeanine next to me. I hadn't had such good sleep in ages, and I would defend to the death my current position.

"Go away," I said waving my arm to ward off the person assaulting my sleep.

"Kane, get the fuck up. Rise and shine."

Oh hell, it's Ryker. I don't know why I listen to that cranky old bastard, especially since he wants me to get up and go to work.

"Let me finish my wellness check of Jeanine," I mumbled.

"Get up," said Ryker. He yanked at my collar which then cut into my throat.

"Okay, okay," I choked out, as I rolled on the raft away from Jeanine. This just wasn't fair. And my jaguar agreed, but hell, as we say in the SEALs the only easy day was yesterday.

"What's the sit-rep?" I asked.

"Do you see a change?" growled Ryker. "Still in the middle of the ocean. Still haven't seen another ship." He pushed a flare gun in my hands. "You know what to do with this."

"Light up my world?"

"Don't stick your pecker too far over the side. The sharks are looking for a little snack."

"Yeah, yeah," I groused as I watched Ryker settle in next to Jeanine and wished it was me instead of him. Damon sat at the other end of the raft with his head lolled to the side. He was out for the duration leaving me alone with my thoughts.

Gunner and Ryker had talked loud enough before I fell asleep, at least for someone with shifters ears, to catch Ryker's rumination on our situation. One woman, four guys? That's overcrowded. But what the hell, it's not like I hadn't done a threesome. What's a couple more bodies? Could be fun.

"Kane?"

Jeanine's sweet voice floated toward me.

"Yeah, babe?"

"You the only one awake?"

"Yep. We're trained to catch sleep when we can."

"You are?"

"No. But as a practical matter, when we're beat-ass tired, it's not that hard to do."

"Kane. You guys are weird."

"How so?"

"Well, for one I've got two men hanging on me."

"Is that a bad thing? They are trying to keep you warm."

"And you guys growl and purr like cats. That's weird."

She was right. I couldn't deny it. We weren't normal men, hence the current situation. But what could I tell her?

Jeanine added, "I feel sick to my stomach. I think it's the rubber and glue smell of the raft."

"How about some jerky? You need food."

"No. That sounds horrible. The boat rocking on the waves doesn't help."

"I think I have some sea sickness pills here."

"You mean Dramamine? That makes me sick to my stomach too."

"Well," I said as I fished one from my pack, "you need to take it. Dehydration from vomiting in the middle of the ocean is dangerous. Besides, it will relax you and put you to sleep."

"I think I've slept enough. And what's with these guys on either side?"

I leaned forward. "Open your mouth and lift your tongue." I spoke in my best, "I'm the medic, so do what I say" tone. She glared at me but did as I asked, and I slipped a tablet under her tongue.

"Now let the pill dissolve, and the medicine will ease your stomach."

She mumbled, and I shook my head.

"Wait until it has melted. You need as much of the Dramamine as possible."

Her nose twitched as she raised an eyebrow. That combination struck me as the cutest thing I'd ever seen.

"Okay," she said. "It's melted. Do we have water? That stuff tastes foul."

"It does. The bitterness doesn't help," I said, handing her a bladder from my backpack. "Survival tip. Wet your lips, mouth and tongue first then swallow. Try not to take more than a swig or two. We don't know how long we've gotta make this last."

She took only two swigs. Her restraint made me proud. My team was used to these survival measures, but she had to pick them up and apply them on the fly. It was a small thing, but it took discipline to drink two swallows when you wanted to down the whole thing.

"Thanks," said Jeanine as she passed the bladder back to me. "So, you guys are used to floating on a raft in the middle of the ocean?"

"We've trained for this contingency, but no, it's not a usual occurrence."

"What situations do you guys get into?"

"Holy hell," grumbled Damon. "Can't a guy get some sleep?"

A snarky remark died on my lips as I caught the drone of an airplane engine. At once, the rest of my team stirred with the whip-quick reflexes of our feline natures and eyes strained into the pre-dawn dark.

"Fire that thing!" growled Ryker.

I pointed into the sky and pulled the trigger. The flare shot into the dark, blazing in an arc in the gray dawn until it faded out. The airplane's engine grew farther away.

"Did they see us?" Jeanine asked hopefully.

"There's no way to know," Ryker explained as the raft rocked to the rhythm of the waves. "We'll just have to wait until someone comes back."

"How do you guys take this?" she huffed.

"We're adrenaline junkies," said Gunner.

"Yeah," deadpanned Damon. "We live for danger."

"Oh, brother," said Jeanine.

"Let's get to work," snapped Ryker. "Damon, pull up the raft survival kit and deploy the solar stills."

"Aye, chief."

"Gunner, deploy the sea anchor."

"Yes, chief."

"Kane, inventory the food."

"Okey-dokey."

"What do you want me to do?"

"You can sit and look beautiful, doll," said Gunner.

"Please," she scoffed.

Ryker handed her the flare gun.

"You can keep watch for passing planes and boats. If you see one, send up a flare."

"Now, listen up. You all know that hygiene is important on a raft. Jeanine, it's a small space, and relieving yourself won't be easy. You can either hang over the side, or take a swim and do the job, but whatever you do, we'll be here to give you a hand."

"And anything else," said Gunner. Most of the time we liked his jokes, or at least put up with them, but now I just wanted to knock his head off.

"Damn it, Rhodes, keep it professional," snarled Ryker. "Things are tense enough on a raft with five people."

"Yes, sir," Gunner intoned, and Ryker's eye's narrowed. Gunner did that on purpose because as we all knew, we did not call non-commissioned officers "sir."

"Hey," said Jeanine. "There's one of me and four of you, and I can't expect you boys to change your raffish ways just because I'm here. Just keep your hands to yourself, and I'll deal with the rest, okay?"

"Well then," said Gunner. "I do have to take care of a piece of business." He pulled up on his knees and unzipped his pants.

"Don't forget to take it in spurts," said Ryker.

"What are you? My mother?"

"Wait," Jeanine said. "What?"

"It's to avoid attracting sharks," said Damon to Jeanine. "We need to make sure we let our pee dilute, so sharks don't pick up the scent."

"Holy hell," said Jeanine. "And I'm supposed to go swimming to do my business?"

"Don't worry," grinned Gunner over his shoulder. "We'll pull you out before you lose a foot or a hand."

"Fuck you, Gunner," I said. He worked my last nerve. "Can't you tell she's frightened enough as it is?"

"I thought laughter was the best medicine, Doc."

"Not when it causes your team to throw you over the side," said Damon.

"Okay, okay," groused Gunner. He turned toward the sea to attend to his private business, which we all had to do.

"And," added Ryker, "let's pull the oars and rig a sunscreen. Do we have a tarp?"

Ryker kept us busy organizing our survival and making things more comfortable. Damn Gunner even had a pair of sunglasses in his backpack. We passed them around to the person doing lookout. The two solar stills, which looked like triangular beach balls, bobbed in the water trailing the raft. These things worked damned slow. So while we had water now, by the time we needed more, we would have a few quarts. But Ryker looked grim. It was not that we couldn't survive out here, but Jeanine concerned us all. We knew what could come, but she didn't.

We could fish and get food that way, but it would be sailor's sushi all the way. And we could only eat if we had enough water because there was nothing worse than dehydration clogging up the pipes. Staying healthy was job one in ocean survival. And that's hard when you contend with sun and salt. Our lips hadn't cracked yet, and our skin hadn't dried by the relentless salt in the water splashing over the sides. But that would happen if we were out here long enough.

Gunner was always problem solving, and fashioned a sea anchor from his backpack and saved the dinky plastic cone masquerading as a raft sea-anchor to scoop out the sea water. When Jeanine licked her lips while his arms scooped and tossed water over the side I reached for a water bladder to hand to her when I caught the gleam in her eye. Yeah, her tongue sliding on her pink lips signaled hunger not thirst and not for food.

What could I do to get her to look at me like that?

Yeah, I'd heard Gunner and Ryker discussing the "sharing the mate" thing. I didn't like it, but neither did challenging my brothers-in-arms tickle me. And it wasn't as if Jeanine was giving any of us the green light, even if she cast covert lustful glances. Women found us irresistible, and that's not a boast. You could call it pheromones or animal magnetism, but we weren't lonely in port if we wished for company.

And Holy Hell—mate? Now that's a concept. When did I ever think of one woman as mine? Never. Marriage, kids, and the-white-picket-fence, were not in my lexicon of life choices. I figured I'd go down in a blaze of glory, fighting the good fight. Now there was a woman in my life even if she didn't realize it. Besides, there was the whole shifter thing. What would she think when she learned of our true nature? That would be a shit storm right there.

One time, about three years ago when we were on leave in Calcutta, a woman saw my animal form. She didn't mention she was married. When her husband walked in and yelled, I was so startled I shifted. Then she screamed loud enough to make my ears ring. I jumped through the closed window smashing it to pieces. But slinking through a back alley with paws filled with tiny pieces of glass was not fun. And removing the shards out of my paws was a bitch. Ryker sucks as a medic. But he was the only one I could turn to, and he did the job, though I'm sure he was rough on purpose to teach me a lesson. But it taught me to be careful about not shifting in front of regular humans. So, four horny cats and one woman unaware of shifters would not make for fun times.

A bump under the raft jolted us.

"What was that?" Jeanine asked. Her eyes were wide, and my ears caught the uptick of her heart.

"Big fish," said Damon.

"What sort of big fish?" she said with her eyes narrowed.

"In the middle of the ocean could be anything," said Ryker noncommittally.

"Dolphins," said Damon.

"Sturgeon," said Ryker.

"Sharks."

"Sharks?" Her voice shot up an octave.

DAMON

*D*amn it. Kane better shut his mouth.

Gunner might be our number one jokester, but Kane was our second. *How dare he upset Jeanine?* If there was a back alley around, I'd take him to it and pound some sense into him.

"Look," I said as I edged closer to her. "Chances are, it's not sharks. Fish get curious when they see something floating on the surface."

"That's a crock," she said.

"No," said Ryker. "It's not."

"Shark attacks are very rare," That was the truth and I tried to say it as reassuringly as possible.

Another bump on the underside of the raft caused her to jump, and she landed in my arms. Or rather, I reached for her and pulled her in. Even after a night on the water, with salt crusted on her skin, she smelled delightful, and the crush of her body against mine made my cat rumble with approval.

"Why do you guys do that?" she said breathlessly. "The purring part I mean."

Her blue eyes drew me like a magnet, and she felt "right"

in my arms in a way no woman had. My chest warmed, and I breathed in her scent with another deep draw. My desire stirred, hardening. I heard the thudding of her heart and caught a whiff of the cream between her legs that said she wanted me.

Mine.

My cat, stuffed deep inside for so much of my life, now hovered right below the surface, infusing his wild thoughts with my rational ones. It was instinctual, this thought, that this woman in my arms belonged to me.

Ryker cleared his throat, and I lifted my head to meet his glare. "Bail the water," he groused. "The raft has to be dry, or you know what will happen."

"What will happen?" said Jeanine.

"Salt sores," I said. "Not pleasant."

"That's not the only thing that's not pleasant here so get moving."

"Aye, aye, *sir,*" I said.

Ryker growled because he hated when any of us called him "sir." Because he was a noncommissioned officer, and we shouldn't, but we did it to yank his chain, which today appeared shorter than usual.

"Well, darling—" I said loosening my grip, but then a shadow fell over the raft, and water splashed as the great fish flew over us.

Many things happened at once.

Jeanine screamed and with my cat so close to the surface of my thoughts, the primal instinct to protect my mate overtook my good sense. I leapt toward the creature, causing the raft to wobble in the water. Ryker swore, Kane dove to throw himself over Jeanine, and Gunner whipped out a handgun. His eyes were wide as he watched my body lengthen, my muzzle form, and my fangs flash. I slammed into the gargantuan fish, not sure what I connected with, but the concussive force of head meeting muscle caused my ears to ring. It fell back into the water, and I went over the side and clamped onto to it. The fish's blood filled my mouth and spilled into the water as red puffs. I hung onto as it thrashed by digging my claws in until it finally went limp. Lifeless, it floated upward, and I went with it.

With the tail of my prize in my mouth and proud of it, I surfaced only to hear Jeanine screaming, and the frantic voices of teammates trying to calm her.

"What the fuck was that! No! Don't lie to me. No! You bastards."

Oh hell, I'd frightened her, and I felt sick. What she saw we should explain, though Gunner tried to feed her some bullshit line about the sun hitting her eyes wrong.

"I know what I saw. Damon changed! Into a cat! What the hell? Oh, fuck. Get off me. Let me off this boat. Oh, hell. Oh, holy hell."

Her panic stroked my protective nature, and I wanted to make this right for her. I shifted, hating myself for my stupidity, and swam to the raft through the water. The blood of that fish would draw sharks, and I didn't want to be their dinner.

I reached the raft and hung my arms over and noticed the raft walls were no longer tight.

"Hey! The raft is leaking!" I called.

Ryker turned to me, swore and barked orders to Gunner to find the leak and fix it. Water sloshed over the weakened side, and Kane rushed to bail it out while Ryker stayed by Jeanine's side talking to her in a low voice. He projected his natural calming presence and held her chin to make her gaze into his eyes. She stopped screaming, but her breathing remained ragged, and her eyes were wide as she stared at him.

Gunner frantically pressed his hands on different

sections of the wall of the raft and found where it collapsed because of the leak. After swiping the area around the hole with an alcohol swab from the medical kit, he slapped a patch with glue over the hole. He pressed on it while the glue dried and at least the raft stopped losing air.

I bobbed in the waves and Gunner waved me over and held out the end of the inflation tube connected to the raft.

"Go at it," he said.

"Me?'

"It was your claw that punctured the raft, idiot." He said the first part slowly, so she hopefully wouldn't overhear. "And get at it so we can haul you into the raft before sharks arrive."

"Sharks," squeaked Jeanine.

Ryker spoke to her in his calm Alpha voice, and she stopped speaking although her gorgeous eyes still sported worry lines. He rubbed her back, and my gut clenched with the green-eyed monster. Why does he get to touch her while I'm stranded in the drink? Well, I'm not stranded, but no one offered me a hand since Ryker's attention centered on Jeanine and Kane bailed seawater.

"Be quiet," I said. "Can't you see how upset she is?"

"And who did that, bro?"

"Shut up."

"You too. And blow."

Gunner put another inflation tube to his mouth, and between us, we huffed to re-inflate that raft section. Something bumped my legs, and I swore.

"It's time to get me out of the water," I said.

"Naw, you haven't stewed enough."

"Dude, there are visitors here."

"Good," said Gunner stubbornly. He went back to huffing on the tube.

"What the hell?" I said.

"Kane," said Ryker, "help Damon."

"No, no, no," babbled Jeanine.

"Shh, darling, shh," said Ryker.

My gut twisted because I caused this. Jeanine was in a bad state because I hadn't held back my cat. And I didn't blame her. What kind of person wouldn't be concerned, after seeing a man turn into a jungle animal. She must think she's crazy and it definitely wasn't the way I wanted to break the truth to her.

Much like I thought when I'd experienced blackouts in my teens, and the police found some poor animal gutted. But the worst was waking in the morning half-naked with no pants, and dried blood under my fingernails. The blood on my ripped and torn t-shirts freaked me out. I didn't know what would have happened if Lieutenant Rogers hadn't shown up and told my parents about a special entry program into the Navy for gifted teens. They didn't want me to go, but they worried about my frequent disappearances at night that they couldn't control. Hell, *I* couldn't control them. My adoptive parents relinquished my care to the tender mercies of the Navy. At least that's what they thought.

But I hadn't met my cat until Ryker came along, and the Navy doctors showed me the tape of what had happened.

Took a while to process that.

I mean, a very long while. I almost scrubbed out though now I'm not sure what that would've meant. You can't have a teenager who shifts into a jungle cat running around on his own. But when Gunner and Kane arrived too, I came around.

You could say they saved my life.

I wanted to help Jeanine process this. It was important because if she was to accept me, *accept us*, she'd have to wrap her head around what we were.

Kane gave me his arm and hauled me over the edge of the

slippery raft. Jeanine stared at me wide-eyed, and her teeth chattered.

"What, what are you?" she said.

Ryker stopped rubbing her back and sat on his heels.

"You mean, what are we?"

"We?" Jeanine whispered, her voice strained as if stretched tight.

Gunner turned and put his hand on her knee.

"We are all like Damon."

"All?" She stared at us with wide eyes. "No, no, no," she babbled and then turned and went to launch herself over the side.

"Oh, no," said Ryker. We all dove for her and grabbed a piece of her as she shrieked in her fright.

"Let me go! Let me go!" she screamed.

"Shh, shh," Ryker said using his Alpha voice to calm her. But it didn't work. She thrashed under their grip.

"Let her go," I said.

"But—"

"Where's she going to go, eh? In the ocean? After she's seen what's in the water?"

Jeanine stilled, as reason dawned and the guys released their grip. She whipped around and faced me with a fierce look on her face, as if she'd take me on and take me down too.

She looked terribly cute at that moment.

"What?" she retorted. "What are you smiling at?"

That she directed her attention to me made me stupidly happy.

"You," I said.

She crossed her arms and huffed.

"You didn't answer my question?"

"He's a jaguar shifter."

"Shi—what? You turned into a big cat?"

"Yep."

She turned again as if to launch herself over the side, but this time Ryker caught her around the waist.

"Stop. No one will hurt you."

"That's right, baby," said Gunner. He sidled next to her. "We want to protect you."

"I don't understand what's happening. I must be hallucinating. That's it. Maybe I bumped my head, and I'm unconscious, and you are all products of my overactive imagination?"

Ryker shook his head. "No, doll, you aren't imagining anything."

"Ha," she huffed. "I'm sure my unconscious mind will say anything to get me to keep this delusion going."

"It might," conceded Kane, "if you were unconscious but you aren't."

She pointed a finger at Kane. "You're a delusion."

"Now, babe," said Gunner.

"Don't 'now babe' me. The only thing that makes sense is that I'm unconscious or dreaming. I don't know what's going on here but grown men do not turn into jaguars."

"We do," said Ryker.

"All of you?"

"Yes," said Kane. "We do."

"Oh, no. No. This can not be happening," she babbled.

Ryker directed Gunner to get the bottle of whiskey he found on our abandoned boat, and he opened it and handed it to her.

"Drink this."

This ethnically wasn;t a good idea, especially in the heat of day, and with limited water supplies. But sometimes you measure one risk against another.

Jeanine gripped the bottle with shaking fingers and took first one swig, then another.

"Ugh," she said.

"What?" said Gunner with a quirky smile. "You don't like our whiskey?"

She took another and pointed her fingers at us.

"What the hell?"

"At least we got past 'no, no, no,'" said Gunner with a smile. She shot him a nasty look, and I didn't blame her. Gunner's smart mouth often got us in trouble.

"Drink some more," urged Ryker.

"Nope, you take a swig now," she said shoving the bottle at him. "You'll drink, and everyone else too."

Ryker sucked on his lips. Like the rest of us, he knew the danger of drinking alcohol on short water rations. But he also wanted to keep her calm.

"Okay," he said, taking the bottle. He passed it to Gunner who took a swig and passed it Kane, who gave it to me. I handed it back to her, but she shook her head.

"Okay, spill. What are you guys? Some weird government science experiment?"

"No," rumbled Ryker. "This is top secret stuff. We shouldn't tell you but considering..."

"Considering what?"

"We'll get to that. From what we can figure, we were born this way. We didn't even know what we were until the government brought us together."

"Ryker," said Gunner, "thinks that our people lived in greater numbers before humans spread over the earth."

"Right," she said with skepticism. "You'll forgive me for not believing you." Her stubborn jaw set, and I wanted to kiss that recalcitrance from her magnificent lips.

"What?" said Kane. "Government experiments to create a race of men who shift into cats is more believable?"

"It might be."

"Well, forget it," said Kane. "No one has the technology to make those kinds of hybrids."

"Chimeras," she said. "That's what they are called."

"Human chimeras, hybrids, what you call them, they aren't possible."

"Didn't some scientists create pig-human hybrids?"

Kane shuddered. "Embryos implanted into pigs, and they destroyed them after four weeks' gestation. It was to see if they could use pigs to grow human organs for transplant. But that's very different from what we are."

"Which is?" said Jeanine.

"Grown men," said Gunner.

"Who happen to shift into jaguars," said Ryker.

I bit my lip. *What the hell am I supposed to think?* As a journalist, this was the biggest story ever to fall into my lap, but if what they said was true, good luck trying to get sources to verify it. It was a crackpot story that belonged in grocery store tabloids, where of course people would say it was a hoax.

And I disliked the way they stared at me, like I was lunch and dessert at the same time. *If they get hungry enough will they snack on me?*

"Take another sip," said Ryker.

"Why? Trying to get me drunk?" I lifted my head to give him a defiant stare.

He shook his head. "No. I want you to steady your nerves because you're freaked out right now."

"You...want...me? What are you? My father?" This was getting out of control. *God help me, someone better come rescue me from these freaks.*

"No," he rumbled dangerously. "Your Alpha."

I swallowed hard at the command in his voice and almost

fell back against the wall of the raft, but then straightened my spine.

"Listen, mister, I don't know what you mean by that, and I don't particularly care. You aren't anything to me, and talk to me again like that, and I'll swat your nose. And let me tell you." I held up my hand and showed my acrylic nails which were long and sharp. "This kitten has claws!"

I did my best to sound threatening, and something worked, though not in the way I expected. Gunner opened his mouth and laughed.

"Hey, Ryker, looks like Kitten put you in your place."

"Shut up, Gunner."

Damon and Kane laughed into their hands, and Ryker's eyes blazed. In fact, they glowed a bright green, which caused me to sit back again. Holy hell, I did not know what I was dealing with.

"You're scaring her," said Damon. "And this won't get us anywhere." He turned to me. "Do you want something to eat?"

I shook my head. My nerves sparked queasiness in my stomach, and I couldn't bear a single thing. In fact, the whiskey wasn't helping my stomach either.

Kane fished in a backpack and brought up another Dramamine tablet.

"Open your mouth and put this under your tongue."

"Those taste awful."

"Not as bad as vomit," said Kane pragmatically.

I wasn't sure, but then Kane hadn't led me wrong yet, and he'd protected me.

"Okay," I said reluctantly. He placed the tablet under my tongue, and I noticed all the men gazing at me.

"Stop that," I said. Or tried to, my words made unintelligible by the tablet.

"Stop what, kitten?" said Gunner. He edged closer to me.

"Staring at me like I'm dinner."

"Oh, he can't," said Damon. "Because you are delicious."

Oh hell, they're going to make a meal out of me. I scrambled backward, my heart rattling and my mouth and throat dry.

"Back off," ordered Ryker. "Damn it! Give her space."

"Right, on a raft," said Gunner caustically.

"I swear to fucking God, if you don't back off I'll toss you in the ocean."

"Okay, okay," Gunner groused. "It's just that it's difficult."

"Yeah," said Kane.

"He's right," said Damon.

I didn't understand what was going on here. Four men who turn into cats wanted to get near me, and I was entirely too freaked out to think rationally about this.

Then I felt another bump under the raft, and again, and my heart tore at my chest it was beating so fast, and I could barely breathe.

"Oh shit," said Kane. "Jeanine, cup your hands over your mouth and nose, and breath."

"What's going on?"

I didn't know who spoke.

"She's hyperventilating."

Ryker slid in next to me on the raft and cupped his large hands over mine and brought them to cover my mouth and nose.

"Breathe deeply," he growled.

His gravelly voice cut through my panic, and I stared into his eyes as he held his hand steady while I sucked in my breath. Finally, my rattling heart slowed and my breathing returned to normal. And I noticed that his eyes held something I hadn't spotted before with all the kissing and groping yesterday. It was honest care and concern.

"That's right," he said reassuringly. "That's good. Relax. I'll take care of you." He peered deeply into my eyes, and I felt the truth of what he said. The sincerity of his words cut through my lingering jitters. He would. Ryker had done nothing less the entire time I'd been with him.

"But why would you?"

A blush crept up his neck, which I did not expect from the rough and tough Ryker.

"Well, here's the thing," said Gunner.

"Quiet, Gunner," snarled Ryker.

"Hey look," cried Kane. "Land Ho!"

Ryker's head whipped to the direction Kane pointed. Mine did too, but I couldn't see anything but a blur on the horizon.

"Maybe we caught a break here," he mumbled.

At once they tore down the canopy they'd constructed earlier and plied the re-purposed oars to the water.

"Pull up the anchor," said Ryker.

"You mean my backpack?" said Damon. "Someone owes me a new one."

"Don't be such a pussy," said Gunner.

The guys snickered at the obvious joke, and I rolled my eyes. I scanned the horizon again, and the blur grew sharper, and I imagined I saw palm trees.

"Is it inhabited?" I asked.

"It probably is," said Ryker.

I swallowed hard. "By what people?"

"Makes no difference," announced Ryker. "Landing will get us out of this raft and on solid ground. From there we can recon."

"Don't worry," said Gunner as his strong arms pulled on the oar. "This is what we do." I watched as the men's muscles flexed and pulled and my stomach fluttered.

"Hmm," I said. Ahead I could barely make out an island, and I wondered how they could be so sure.

"What these guys aren't saying," said Kane, "is that the

sailors trawled the Caribbean for five hundred years at least, not counting the natives. This is all well-traveled, more like your everyday neighborhood than the wild mid-Atlantic. We haven't seen a ship in the aftermath of the storm, but if we hung out another day, someone would run into us."

"If it weren't for your propensity to jump ship, we'd just hang out."

"Yeah, drinking whiskey." I snorted.

"And eating fisherman's sushi," said Gunner with a wink. "What guys don't like to hang out, drink and fish?"

I rolled my eyes. "You make a joke of everything, don't you, Gunner? I'm sure if we were drowning you'd make a joke of that too."

"Anything to keep up morale," said Gunner.

"Who made you morale officer?" said Damon.

"First, take back those nasty words. I'm not an officer. Second, I *volunteered.*"

This set the other three men laughing, and I didn't understand the joke. I sat and crossed my arms.

"What?" said Kane.

"I don't get the joke."

"No one volunteers. Officers do that for us," said Gunner with a big grin.

I shook my head. What the hell have I gotten into? Sure, they were hot; I could melt just looking at any of them. Ryker with his muscles and dark eyes. Gunner, blond, tan, and succulent; Kane, with his chestnut hair and green eyes; and Damon with his blue-black hair and blue eyes. They were all delicious.

But they weren't human. *Shifters? Jungle cats?*

No, I can't process it. Damon changed before my eyes, and I still couldn't believe it. I'd rather chew on Ryker's lie that the sun got into my eyes.

But I'm a journalist, damn it—dedicated to the truth, and

sometimes you just have to look at the stark naked version and put it out there. *But how do I tell this story without looking like a lunatic?*

No way, that's how.

However, I still needed to find my friend, Surma, and learn her fate. I couldn't accept she was dead and needed to see the evidence if she was. I had to get back to St. Lucia and track down Aedan Morgan. It would be harder, now that my cover was blown, but I'd manage. All I had to do was to escape from these guys, however impossibly sexy they were, and I'd attack my mission once again.

The island loomed larger, and when we moved closer to shore, we saw an expanse of white-sand beach and a tropical forest rising above it.

"Where are we?"

"Not sure yet. One of the islands," said Gunner. He had pulled out the satellite phone and stared at the GPS.

"An island," snorted Kane. "That's informative."

"Doesn't do much good without a map, does it?" sniggered Damon.

"You guys rag on each other constantly, don't you?"

"Oh, yeah," said Ryker.

"It shows how much we love each other," sneered Gunner.

They were more relaxed as we got closer to land, and they'd lost their grim expressions. The tropical forest became a solid wall of green straight ahead, and a jut of land rose on the left covered in scrubby bushes. The closer we got to the beach, the crashing of the waves on the shore became louder. We bobbed in the surf, and then they jumped out and dragged the raft up on the shore.

"Okay, recon," said Ryker. "Let's figure out what country we're in and who we need to call. Gunner, Kane, Damon, spread out, and find some landmarks."

"Right, Chief," said Gunner, and they sprinted off into the jungle.

"Landmarks?"

"All the islands in the region are inhabited and occupied by some country. The ocean currents sweep north, and we weren't at sea long enough to drift toward Venezuela, so I'm guessing we've hit either Martinique or the Dominican Republic."

Good. Either island was not too far from St. Lucia. First, I'd find a U.S. Embassy to get an emergency passport and scare up a new debit card. Then, I'd catch local transport back to St. Lucia after I said adios to the cat people who would have to go back to the military.

See? Easy. No probs.

Then why was my gut shredded? This was ridiculous. I barely knew these men.

But you feel Ryker's lips against yours. Gunner's mouth on your spine, his hard cock against you. Damon and Kane holding you warm and tight after the worst day of your life. Sure, it was unconventional but why wouldn't you like that?

This couldn't be happening. I buried my toes in the warm wet sand and stared at the air bubbles rising from it as the ocean pulled and washed over this sliver of shore. The water here was a gorgeous blue. I sat on the sands of paradise and I couldn't lie. Land, any land felt good right now but the beauty of the island wasn't lost on me despite everything we'd gone through.

My mind wandered back. Four men at once. Nope. That was insane enough. But four shifter men who turned into cats? Even crazier.

Sand grating startled me from my reverie, and I lifted my head to meet Ryker's eyes as he pulled the raft more firmly onto the shore. His mouthwatering muscles bunched as he pulled the plastic beast out of the water and toward me.

His mouth on mine. Questing. Eager. Possessive.

My face flushed with these thoughts, and the less ladylike part of me tingled, eager for more of his touches.

No. I must stop thinking this way.

I shaded my eyes with my hand to stay meeting his gaze.

"Will they remain away long?" I said.

Ryker huffed as he dropped the raft.

"They'll be back," he said. "I'd go with them…"

"But someone has to watch me? That's a load of bull."

Ryker's eyes and mouth creased with worry lines, and I recognized this expression as his prelude to laying down the law.

"We are in unknown territory with unknown hostiles."

"Bull. We're in the Caribbean. All I need to do is find the American Embassy, and I can work things out on my own."

Now Ryker's mouth twisted in extreme dislike.

"Is that what you want?"

"What else would I want? Hey, it's been a fun adventure, but I've got a life, you know. And an employer. It's time I went home." I'm not sure what he's asking me, but it's high time I got off the train to crazy town.

Ryker squatted before me and took my hand.

"I can't let you do that," he said.

I'm going insane.

When Jeanine said she wanted to leave and go home, my cat growled deep inside me. My heart flip-flopped. It'd been a long time since it performed gymnastics like that. My gut clenched.

Without realizing it, I bent before her and took her hand.

"I can't let you do that."

Which apparently was the wrong thing to say because she snorted derisively and twisted her lips in disbelief.

"So, you're going to keep me prisoner?"

The challenge in her voice snapped me to the sickening reality. If she didn't want to stay with me—with us, what could we do that wouldn't break the law?

Persuade her, said my cat.

A low growl rumbled in my gut that I could not contain, and her gorgeous blue eyes flew open in surprise. Jeanine scooted backward.

"Don't do that," I pleaded.

"You growled. Cats growling signals a threat." She stared

at me fiercely, and I melted. Then I said something I rarely do.

"Sorry."

"You are?" she said with skepticism.

"Yeah. It's just…well…I…we…" I lowered my head, clueless as to what to say. How did you explain to a woman you just met that she's your forever mate? It sounded insane even to me, who long ago got used to the quirky nature of my blended selves.

Jeanine laughed then, and my head snapped up again.

"What?"

"You're all tongue-tied."

My face flushed. *Damn it.* This woman turned my head around. I was the Alpha here, and one small woman should not turn my guts inside out.

Even if she did.

"You do that to me," I admitted. "Look, this is uncharted territory for me."

"Hmm, so does that mean you expect danger to pop out at us any moment?"

"It could. We aren't sure where we are or what government we're dealing with. If law enforcement takes us into custody, we're cooked. The brass will disavow us, and we must do whatever to keep our mission secret."

"Even if they imprison you?"

"Wouldn't be the first time."

She shook her head. "Why do you do it then? The special ops stuff must be dangerous."

"It's what we do."

"That's not a good answer, Ryker."

I sat next to her and gazed out at the ocean.

"I suppose once I learned I was a freak, I thought the usual stuff, a wife, home, and kids, was out of my reach."

"Don't call yourself that. You're not a freak."

"Yeah? You didn't seem to think that when Damon changed in front of you."

She shrugged. "You guys surprised me."

"Yeah, but what woman wants a man that's part cat? And a dangerous one at that? Who will say, 'yeah, baby, come here and make some kittens with me?'"

Jeanine blew out a puff of air.

"Tell me something, Ryker. What were you like as a kid?"

I shrugged. "Just like any other."

"And you didn't know what you were?"

"No. When things got strange when I was a teenager, the military came for me."

"Hmph. Just like that?"

"I guess."

"And you didn't get that people were watching you so that when you started showing your spots, they conveniently arrived to scoop you up?"

I scratched my head. I didn't think of it that way, but I was messed up then from the weird things happening to me. To tell the truth, I was glad they let me enlist even though it was earlier than I should have.

"So what if they did? They did me a favor."

Jeanine made a rude noise through her nose.

"Yeah, and they got a team of jaguar shifters together to do their dirty work. I think they should be grateful to you."

Anger edged her voice, and that she got angry for me instead of at me warmed my heart. Then she gripped my hand.

"You shouldn't blame yourself for what you are. You aren't a freak, Ryker. Just different. You have the right to anything due to a man in this world."

For a brief second a swell of hope bloomed in my chest. Perhaps things weren't that bad. She could reconsider going home and explore what she might have with us.

"But you can't keep me a prisoner, Ryker. Like I said, I have a life."

She can have a life with us.

My cat was damned persistent while the human part of me understood. What sane woman ditched her life to spend it with four men? But cats weren't known for their reasoning skills though they excelled in the relentless pursuit of their prey.

Jeanine squeezed my hand and tried to release it. Instead, I pulled her to my chest, and my cat purred in approval. She made a small noise but relaxed against me.

The fragrance of her hair filled my nose, and I put my arm around to hold her to me. This was exactly what I needed, and I didn't want to move in case she used the opportunity to draw away.

If I could, I wouldn't ever let her pull away again.

Persuade her.

My cock found Jeanine in my arms enticing, and it stirred from holding her tight to my body.

"You feel good in my arms," I whispered in her ear. I unbuckled her life vest with one hand. "Let's get this off you."

"I think I'm safer if I keep it on."

"Are you?" I said as I pulled her onto my lap. I immediately got hard, and my length pressed into her delectable bottom. My hand slipped under the vest, and I cupped and squeezed her breast while licking behind her ear. She meowed, and her breasts rose and fell with her quickening breaths. Her flesh was deliciously salty, her unique taste and arousal scented the air between us. My hardness pulsed with need.

"Look, um, we're on a beach here. Who knows who's looking?"

"You're right," I said, and I stood sweeping her into my arms, and ran for the water."

"What?" she shrieked and laughed, and my legs plowed into the water. I twisted and fell into the waves, clasping her.

She struggled, but I stood upright with water cascading off of us, never letting her go. My heart raced, and all I wanted was to get closer to her.

"I've got you," I said.

"Yes, and we're fully dressed."

"The clothes needed a wash anyway," I said smiling.

"Is that how you do your laundry? In salt water?"

"We're trained to make things work regardless of the situation," I murmured into her ear. She shivered. The water swirled around us, and the sun beat down warmly with a gentle breeze curling through the cove. I had my woman in my arms, and right now I didn't care if I was on a mission. This was right.

Our eyes met, and the electric connection I felt with her magnified a hundred times. I lowered my head and claimed her mouth while pressing our bodies together. I was not a religious man but kissing her was the closest I'd ever been to heaven.

"Stay and let me take care of you," I breathed into her ears, and she shivered.

But then she put her hands to my chest and pushed away. "But, Ryker, as terrific as you are, I can't stay here and figure out whatever's happening between us. I came to St. Lucia for a reason, and that was to find my friend, Surma. Morgan has her, and I have to do something."

"I told you, we saw no one named Surma. And he had lots of people on his ship."

She bit her lip.

"That can't be the answer. I went through all that trouble to get that information. Wait. All the state stuff I stole, which I planned to use to get her back—that's all ruined from the storm, isn't it?"

"Maybe not," I said. "I put them in my backpack, and those are waterproof."

"You have to help me get her back, Ryker."

My mate is single-minded. What can I do? This had gone way beyond a blown op. We should hitch a ride out of the Caribbean and go for ground. If we could take a second shot at the mission and achieve our objective no one could complain. But could we traipse through the Caribbean and wreak a trail of destruction without making a shit stain of the op? My reasoning mind said no. One of our mottos was "don't run into your own death." To pursue Morgan now would be knocking on death's door.

"Sorry, doll. That's not the mission."

Her eyes narrowed, and she slapped me hard. She was stronger than she looked. Stars blinded me, and her hand stung like hell.

"Bastard!" she said. Jeanine turned and thrashed through the water toward the shore. Before I knew it, she was out and tearing toward the green jungle line.

"Wait!" I called. "You don't know—"

She turned and flipped me off and then sprinted into the tropical forest.

Fuck.

My cat was angry and itched to come out, but I had to keep him shielded from potentially prying eyes.

Hold on. Hold on. We'll catch her.

My feet hit the hot sand. *Where did I lose my shoes?* Probably the same place I put my head. Jeanine was a danger to all sense and logic, and I kicked myself for not seeing that sooner. I was the team leader. It was my job to keep a cool head and the focus on the mission objective. But what did I do? Toss it all for a cuddle and a kiss? What the hell was wrong with me?

Mate, said the cat.

Fuck you.

Right back at you, the beast said in the most lucid speech I'd ever heard in my head. *I've done everything you wanted of me, staying hidden and working when called on. You've pushed our body to the limit and nearly got us killed on multiple occasions. The very least you can do is stop acting like a stupid human male and go after the female who's ours. If you don't, I see no reason to come running when you call.*

Wow. I mean, could that happen? Would the beast fail to manifest when I needed it?

You can't do that.

Try me, human.

That part of me sounded angry, and I couldn't believe I was at war with myself. I mean sometimes the cat pulled me back. Later, I'd found that the situation was unsafe. But this was different.

Occupied with my thoughts, I didn't notice when my feet hit the forest floor. A musty aroma, filled with wet earth, rain and jungle flowers greeted my nose. Above me, animals chittered in the understory and the canopy layers. It was at once both cooler and more humid than the beach. I panicked for a second when the flood of new sensations overwhelmed me, and I couldn't pick up her scent.

I stood surrounded by the underbrush and listened, but all I heard were insects, birds, and monkeys, but no Jeanine. What the hell would I do now?

Cursing, I considered shifting, but I still didn't know how populated this island was and I was not ready to ditch my clothes yet. Finally, I caught Jeanine's scent and followed it, faint as it was. It drew me deeper into the jungle.

Footsteps crashing the underbrush spiked my attention. *Oh, hell. This cannot be good.* My team would not make that amount of noise. *Who are they? What's their intent?* They were moving fast as if alarmed so they couldn't be law enforcement, which would walk the rainforest with deliberation and care.

I came to a small clearing to see Jeanine holding up her hands, with her back to me.

The man pointing the gun at her dripped an aura of danger and ill intent.

So did the man at my back who stuck a gun barrel into my neck.

A few miles into the jungle the green broke onto a one-lane paved road that communicated that civilization of a sort lay nearby. I whistled, and before long my shrill call brought my teammates to my side.

"Yeah," said Kane. "I saw it too."

"When I was up on the ridge," said Damon pointing north, "I saw several boats hugging the shore. There's probably a town there."

"You think?" snorted Kane.

"Man, you are a smart ass," said Damon.

"Nah, that's Gunner."

"No, I've got a smart mouth."

"Makes no difference where the shit comes from, men," said Damon. "It still stinks."

I scoffed.

"What's the move?" I asked Damon. Technically, he was our second-in-command, so both Kane and I waited for his word.

"I say we go back, get Ryker and Jeanine and head north

on the shore. That seems to the closest to what passes for civilization here."

"That's what we want to do?" Kane questioned. "I mean, Morgan is out there and probably put word about that his four bodyguards blew up his ship. And he's got to have help from the locals to pursue his criminal activities."

"What's your problem, Kane? Like we can't handle a few locals?"

"That's not it," said Kane. "We can handle it, but what about Jeanine?"

"Yeah," said Damon.

Oh hell.

We glanced at each other, and the realization hit us at the same time. Our first thought wasn't our mission, but Jeanine's safety.

"Fuck," I said. "This changes everything."

"How do you figure?" said Kane. "We're still us."

"Are we?" said Damon. "When have we ever bombed a mission this badly?"

"Missions go sideways," said Kane.

"And that's not Jeanine's fault," I said. The need to defend her overrode my good sense, because Damon had a point, and my brain knew that. My emotional center, however, did not, and this was disturbing.

"No, but since meeting her, we haven't had the same amount of focus on our mission objectives. That's a problem."

We stared at each other as the immense depth of the shit we were in crashed on us. With Jeanine as our mate, our focus would always be on her. Our lives were now fundamentally changed.

"What are we going to do?"

Damon shook his head. "I don't know. Can we even stay in the service?"

"No," said Kane. "I can't accept that. We worked hard."

"Well, that's just it, isn't it?" I said. "The average length of enlistment for a SEAL is fifteen years, but most of them deploy only a third of that and spend the rest of time pushing paper."

"Yeah," said Damon, "I know that."

"And we've deployed continually for like what? Close to ten years? Add it up. We're past our expiration date."

"If we were fully human," said Kane, "which we're not."

"That's what the DOD depends on."

"Yeah, we're the 'better soldier' they've always wanted."

"Or one form of it," said Damon thoughtfully.

"I think," I said, "it's time to retire."

"And do what?" snorted Kane.

"Work for another security company?"

"Like who?" said Damon.

"I don't know."

"Perhaps we just need to find those other shifters that Ryker says are out there?"

"Perhaps. There is one thing for sure," said Damon. "Jawing is not moving this op forward. Let's go find Ryker."

"And Jeanine," said Kane.

"Yes, Jeanine," said Damon derisively. "She's our North Star now, isn't she?"

Was she? Yes. Damon hit the nail just right.

Damon turned and headed back into the tropical forest, and we fell in side-by-side. Kane muttered which was never a good sign.

"This is not what I signed up for," he said. "What the hell happened? Why?"

"It's not important that you like it," I said spouting a SEAL truism and being a jerk about it. "It's important that you do it."

"Smart ass," he said. "Our creed also says, 'The ability to

control my emotions and my actions, regardless of circumstance, sets me apart from other men.' This doesn't look like control to me."

"Who says biology isn't destiny?" tossed Damon over his shoulder.

"You think this is about biology?" I said.

"Mating? Yeah. Instinctual. Biological," he said definitively. "What do we know about our biology, eh?"

"Cats do not take lifelong mates," said Kane.

"But we aren't a hundred percent cat," said Damon. "Our genetic profile is mostly human."

"How do you know?" said Kane.

"I talked to Dr. Melkot at the facility."

That asshole. Melkot was up our butts every minute of the day while we were there. He oversaw the poking, prodding, and testing of our abilities. I had a big hate-on for that guy and was ecstatic to get out of his range of fire when we went to our first advanced skill training class.

"Humans don't mate for life either," I said.

"Some primates do. And others form strong social bonds."

"Like humans."

"Yes. So what we feel is Jeanine's not so much our mate, as belonging with us?"

"Man," said Kane. "That's too deep for me."

"But it makes sense," I said. "I mean, how she was on Morgan's yacht, that was fearless."

"Yeah," Kane said. "She handled herself well on the yacht. On the raft though..."

"Cut the woman a break," snarled Damon. "She hasn't had our training and was in a raft with four men after a difficult day. I say she performed aces."

"What?" said Kane. "You want to make her a member of the team?"

"You aren't getting it, Kane," said Damon. "She is a member. Period."

"It's not the same," said Kane. "There are no female SEALs."

"Hence the reason we need to retire," I said.

"Fuck," said Kane. His voice communicated his thorough unhappiness with the idea. I couldn't say I blamed him.

Inwardly I seconded his assessment. I'd considered retirement and tossed it around more often the past couple months, but I couldn't fathom leaving these guys behind. It felt unnatural, like I was leaving my family. I tried to tell myself that every birdie leaves the nest, but I couldn't bring myself to fly the coop. Nope, I was in it for the long haul with these guys.

And now Jeanine was in the mix.

"We have a lot to straighten out," I said.

"No sh—" Damon skidded to a stop and threw the arm signal telling us to do the same. On high alert, we halted and strained our ears.

There it was. Men shouting, about a quarter mile away, two minutes ahead.

"¡Las manos en la cabeza. Ponte en el suelo¡"

Hell, someone was in trouble.

"No!" shrieked Jeanine.

Double hell. I growled, and so did Kane, but Damon steadfastly signaled that we hold position. My cat clawed at my skin, eager to get to and help Jeanine, but I had to keep my head as much as the beast in me resisted. I clamped down, sucking in a deep breath and focused on what I needed to do.

Damon gave Kane a signal to spread out to the right, and me left, as he moved forward cautiously, taking point.

Jeanine screamed again, and we crept through the understory of the rainforest. Insects buzzed around us, but the birds and other animals were quiet and lying low, waiting for the danger to pass.

We got close enough to see Ryker sprawled on the ground and blood dripping down his face. Jeanine knelt next to him and glared at the men pointing rifles at her.

"You bastard," she spat. "You didn't need to do that. He surrendered."

"Si," snarled one man. "For now. This guy worked with Señor Morgan on the boat and blew it up. Señor Morgan will be very glad to see him."

With one guy covering an unconscious Ryker and a kneeling Jeanine, Jerk Face kicked Ryker. Jeanine threw herself in front of the kick and received the vicious blow. She uttered a pained sound and clenched her gut.

That did it. Damon raised his hand with the claw sign.

My heart sped as adrenaline surged through me, kicking off the change. Spotted fear sprang as my limbs and face rearranged and reformed. I sniffed the air and found my mate's fear-laced scent and heard my Alpha's regular breathing. He was only acting, probably thinking if he did anything then bullets would fly, which would endanger Jeanine.

I circled to the south, Kane to the north and Damon kept human form to give us directions with bird calls. It must kill him not to go on the attack, but one of us needed to stay human to keep a leash on the rest of us.

I was on one side of the clearing and Kane was on the other.

"Caw!" Damon signaled.

I sprinted and flew into the man holding a gun at my team leader and my mate and brought him down. Damon took out the other man. Both screamed like babies and swore in Spanish. I couldn't resist tearing a small amount of flesh from his shoulder and savored the small trickle of blood I lapped up. It was barely a scratch, but he pleaded to God and begged for his life ,but the only God here was the jaguar God, and he was not pleased.

Damon walked into the clearing toward us and kicked away the men's firearms.

"Are you okay?," he asked Jeanine.

"Yes, but Ryker isn't."

"I wouldn't be sure of that."

Ryker groaned and sat up.

"Took you guys long enough to get here," he said crankily.

"Ryker!" exclaimed Jeanine, and she threw herself into his arms.

"I'm fine."

"No, you were out. You could have a concussion."

Kane chuffed with a feline laugh.

"What?" she said.

"His head is so hard, I'm surprised the butt end of that rifle hasn't cracked," said Damon.

"Go get the backpacks. We shouldn't leave them on the beach anyway."

"Aye, chief," he said, and he sprang into the forest at a run.

"Now," said Ryker to our captives. "You'll tell us who you are, who you work for, and what damned island we're on."

KANE

Our captive refused to cooperate.

Still, in my animal form, I smelled the fear rolling off him, but he must be more afraid of his employer than us.

It was time to change that.

I huffed to get Ryker's attention.

"What do you think, Kane?" said Ryker. "He doesn't want to cooperate."

"Ask him about Surma," said Jeanine coldly. She stared at our captive with narrowed eyes. "She has dark skin and eyes, and black curly hair."

"You," said Ryker. "Do you know anything about a dark-skinned woman hanging around Morgan?"

"No hablo Ingles," he said stubbornly. He stuck out his chin defiantly and stared at us like he wanted to kill each one of us.

"See, Jeanine. He doesn't speak English."

"He understood, 'Hands up, get on the ground' well enough."

"That he did," said Ryker. He glanced at me.

"Kane, you can apply your persuasion skills now."

I stalked toward him, and he tried to crab walk backward, but Ryker stopped him. Eye to eye with our captive, I growled.

"Diablo!" he yelled and then jabbered a long string of Spanish words. Ryker spit at him in Spanish, which only made him more frantic. He tried to twist away from Ryker and then spotted my fangs not two feet from his face. He screamed again when I laid my paw on his shoulder.

The other guy pleaded with him to talk as Gunner pressed his paws on the man's chest. He panted with his large jaguar tongue hanging out of his jaw. The sight of Gunner's fangs terrified the man enough to make him pray to the Blessed Virgin.

They say there are no atheists in foxholes. Apparently, there aren't in a Caribbean rainforest either when a jaguar stares you in the face. Ryker's captive babbled a steady stream of Spanish words. I sniffed the man's neck, and he shrieked before passing out.

"Good job, Kane," said Ryker sarcastically. "We were just getting useful intel from him."

Damon returned and tossed our backpacks to us. They landed with thuds on the ground. Damon pulled a length of rope from his and flipped the unconscious man over and lashed his wrists and ankles.

"Please, señor, do not leave me with the Diablo," said the man I guarded. Por favor," he pleaded.

Jeanine stood and walked to him, and I followed her.

"Why should we?" she said fiercely. "You tried to hurt us, and your employer kidnapped my friend. You better talk now. Otherwise, I'll leave you to my kitties here."

It should offend me she called me a kitty, but she said it with such affection that it warmed my heart. I butted my head into her hip, and absently she scratched behind my ear.

Okay, now I know why cats go nuts for that. It was the best sensation aside from sex, her hand sent waves of pleasure down my spine. What have I've been missing all these years? I got the urge to flop to the ground and show her my cat stomach, but nope, I had to keep on the mission. Still, I head-butted her again after she pulled her hand her away to let her know I wanted to get closer.

She was my mate.

"Kane," snapped Ryker.

Right. I can't act the part of fierce jungle cat when I'm acting like a house cat. I whipped my head back to the man whose eyes widened in fear once again.

"Madre de Dios," he swore.

"Nope," said Ryker. "She's the jaguar goddess coming to call. You've heard of her right? Rules the underworld with her mate? Do you want to see hell? She'll send you there."

The man muttered, and I lunged at him, but Jeanine put her hand on my shoulder, and I stopped. But I growled.

"Tell us what we want to know," she said. "Or I don't think I can hold my kitties back. They're hungry."

"I swear that I don't know nothing," he babbled.

She sighed. "Oh, well. Nice knowing you."

"Wait, wait, Morgan has a base at the marina. He came in last night in a bad, bad mood. Brought a girl with him like you described. She didn't look good."

"Fuck," said Jeanine.

"Where's this marina?" said Ryker.

"Over the ridge, in the harbor, north, ten kilometers."

"On your stomach," ordered Ryker.

"Don't let the cats—" gasped the man.

"Stop stalling," said Damon. He flipped the man face down while our captive took breaths in ragged gasps, and used a torn-up sheet to blindfold him.

"The cats, the cats," he muttered.

I shifted, and Jeanine watched wide-eyed as my fur receded and my jaguar frame reverted to a man. She eyed my naked form appreciatively, which caught Ryker's attention.

"Get dressed," he ordered. "We have work to do."

I pulled out green khakis and a black tee and winked at Jeanine as I pulled them on. She smiled.

"Kane," growled Ryker.

Jeanine took two steps to Ryker and looked up at him. "I appreciate this," she said in a voice that would melt frozen butter, "helping me find Surma."

That did the trick. Oh, this woman had it all over us because Ryker's neck flushed red. He was as gone on her as I was.

Gunner dressed too and flashed a grin at me after he saw Ryker's reaction. Damon looked away, deep in thought, which he did when he was thinking about mission objectives. But what mission he was on, I couldn't guess. He might be on board with finding this Surma chick or trying to find alone time with Jeanine.

"Okay," said Ryker., "Let's head out."

"Don't leave me alone with the cats," said our conscious captive. He squirmed on the ground. Gunner put his hands on the man's shoulders, causing him to start.

"What cats?" he said. Then he growled a long, dangerous, growl which caused the prone man to thrash and scream.

"You've missed your calling," I said. "You should have gone into psy-ops."

"Aww," said Gunner., "I didn't know you cared."

"Enough, you two. Let's get to work."

"What about these guys?" said Jeanine.

"We'll get in touch with local law enforcement and let them know their location," said Ryker.

It took a little over two hours to make it to the marina. We could have gone faster, but the terrain was rough and

Jeanine, as game as she was, didn't usually hike in these conditions. But we did "help" Jeanine during our hike.

Okay, she didn't need our help. But that didn't stop us from offering a hand down steep slopes or swinging her over rocky streams. We competed to see who would get to Jeanine first, and she shook her head with a wry smile as we got more ridiculous.

"Ryker," she called. "Why aren't you reining these guys in?"

"Because," he said. "I'm waiting for my turn. I'll let these other guys tease you. When it's my time, I'll please you."

"Is that right," Jeanine challenged.

"Big words," said Gunner.

"You wait and see," said Ryker with authority. Right, big man. Chief Ryker Hardin, hard ass.

"Maybe you don't get time alone," said Damon.

"That's what you think."

"Now, wait a minute, you make it sound as if you'll share me," said Jeanine.

"That's right," said Damon. He swept her into his arms. "You are part of Team Shadow now."

I was not thrilled that Damon was holding her, and that she was looking at him with wide blue eyes, but hey, she looked at me that way too. So I could be patient. For a little while.

"And who decided that?" said Jeanine.

"We did," I said. "Or rather our cats. They see you as our mate."

"What!" she shrieked. "What does that mean?"

"Quiet," said Ryker peering ahead. "We're getting closer to the marina. We don't want to tip off any of Morgan's men that we're here. At least, not yet."

"Explain to me," she said in a lower but fierce voice, "how I can be mated to each of you."

"We aren't sure," I said. "Damon thinks it's instinctual."

"At some point," said Damon, "we will have to find out more about our origins so we can get a better handle on this. We don't understand from where this comes. But we all want you, so we have to share."

"Really?" she said. "And I have no say in this? And let me down."

Damon put her feet on the forest floor.

"Well, doll," said Ryker. "It's that or a fight to the death, and I'd rather not lose any of my team."

Her face flash with concern as Ryker mentioned death.

"So we decided you were part of the team."

"And how will your superior officers feel about that?"

"After this mission," said Damon, "we won't have superior officers anymore. We're resigning."

Ryker swiveled his head toward Damon.

"We are?" His eyes narrowed. "Who made that decision?"

"We talked about it," said Damon, "after we found the road."

"You didn't tell me about the road," groused Ryker.

"Case in point," said Damon. "We wanted to get back to Jeanine and went in her direction. That will shoot our mission effectiveness all-to-hell, don't you think?"

"Instinctual," growled Ryker.

"Yes," said Gunner. "Think of it, Chief. We can't keep our head on the mission if we're itching to get back to Jeanine, or if we're worried about her safety."

"What do you think about this, Kane?" asked Ryker.

"I don't like it," I said.

"At least you have your head on straight."

"Not exactly. I feel the same way as Damon and Gunner. I just don't have to like it."

Ryker huffed. "Let's get this body snatch done, and we'll talk about it later."

"And what about me? What about my feelings?"

Gunner grinned so wide it was almost a leer.

"Just sit back and enjoy the ride, baby."

"Oh, boy," she said rolling her eyes.

"Don't worry, babe," I said. "I'll save you from that smooth dog."

"What? Do you guys know how to speak English?"

"A smooth dog is a slick talking womanizer," said Damon.

"Hey," said Gunner in an aggrieved voice. "I resemble that remark."

"Quiet," snapped Ryker. Our heads whipped to Ryker who walked point, and he held up his arm to signal we should stop in our tracks. Then he pointed to Gunner to go forward on a sneak-and-peek. Gunner cast Jeanine a rueful glance, then took off forward. Ryker sent me after him.

"Gotta go, babe," I said. "Buddy system, remember?"

"Right," she said.

I took off into the underbrush, following my teammate, and saw what Ryker did. It was a well-worn path that led the rest of the way down the mountain. Beyond the end of it, the blue Caribbean waters sparkled in a small harbor sitting between the folds of high ground. Three docks jutted out from the shore sporting a series of different sized boats, large and small. This would appear perfectly normal except for the men who patrolled the shore with automatic assault rifles hanging off their shoulders. Three mismatched tin-roofed buildings sat further in the fold on the thin sliver of beach.

Gunner touched my shoulder and jerked his head back toward the rest of our team, letting me know we should report what we saw. But then a flash of white came out of one building, and the unmistakable figure of Aedan Morgan lit a cigarette. He stared out toward the water.

I gave the hand sign indicating I'd stay, and Gunner shook his head, leaving me alone to keep an eye on Morgan. If there was one thing we didn't want, it was Morgan hopping on one of those ships.

He paced on the sand and kept looking out toward the head of the harbor, drawing deep drags of his cigarette. He looked worried, but then he should be.

We would come for him soon.

DAMON

Gunner found a cave next to a waterfall buried in the ridge's cleft, and we set up our base there. Ryker wanted a safe place for Jeanine, and with the cave, only one of us needed to stay with her. One backpack held a thermal blanket, and I laid it on the floor of the cave to give her something to sit on.

We decided to wait until night to make our assault and use the dark to our advantage. If we blazed in during the day, then we'd face six men with deadly automatic rifles, a ton of bad attitude and nothing to tip the scales in our favor. Ryker would lead, Kane and Gunner would go in feline form, and I would stay with Jeanine. Yeah, I drew the long straw—literally. Jeanine scoffed when we pulled lots for the privilege of protecting her.

Ryker and Gunner shifted and disappeared to patrol the jungle, and Kane changed to his jaguar self as Jeanine watched wide-eyed. Kane's powerful cat head-butted her as playfully as a house cat. She reached out tentatively to pet his fur, and he chuffed.

"Pretty kitty," she said.

Kane growled. It was a hollow but powerful sound that frightened most people, and she held up her hands in surrender. "Okay. I won't call you a pretty kitty," she said. "But you are cute."

Kane chuffed in annoyance and turned to leave us alone in the cave.

"Looks like I struck a nerve," Jeanine said. She stared after Kane, biting her lip.

"Don't take it personally. He doesn't like the idea of leaving the service."

"You guys don't have to that on my account."

I put my arm around her and drew her to me and kissed the top of her adorable head.

"Sure we do, darling. We can't function like we usually do since we met you, and that could get us killed."

"But it doesn't sound right, or fair."

"We served a decade. If we stuck it out until retirement, we'd have to do another ten years. But I suspect, given our nature, they'll give us a difficult time either way in quitting or retirement. We're part lab rat to them, and they won't let us go willingly."

"Are you sure about that?"

"Yes. They don't treat us the same as other SEALs. We spend more time on missions than other units. When we return to base, which is rare, they segregate us from other soldiers. I'm sure they want to see how many missions we can take before we crack. Maybe it's just time."

"Why? Because the last mission didn't go well?"

"We didn't fulfill our objectives the first time. This time, he won't get away." I spoke with confidence and authority, and she swallowed hard.

I stared intensely into her crystal blue eyes. There were whole worlds there swirling around with new mysteries to explore.

"You aren't used to death, are you?" I said.

"I've seen things. I've just haven't hung out with guys like you who deal with death as a matter-of-course."

"There's nothing casual about our work. It's a job our country needs, and we do it with precision and skill. Besides, who else better to do this than a group of apex predators?"

"I don't know what to think," she said. "And certainly I don't know what to think about all you guys with me. Calling it unusual would the understatement of my life."

"Yeah," I said. I stroked her soft hair and kissed her cheek, but I wanted so much more. "But at least life won't be boring."

"Life? As in my entire life?"

"That's what mate means," I murmured in her ear. "Let me show you how exciting life will be."

"Now?" she said surprised.

"We have hours before we move. I think we can spare a little time for what's important."

She didn't say "no," and that's all I needed. With my hand, I turned her face to mine and kissed her. Nothing felt so right in my entire life as kissing this woman. She was gorgeous, and with the sweetness of her lips, my cock hardened and throbbed. My lips grazed her neck and behind her ears, and she made a noise of want that unleashed my desire. I couldn't get enough of her skin. My fingers undid her bra, and I buried my head in the mound of her breasts, licking, nibbling, and grazing my teeth on her nipples. She moaned under me, and her arousal drove me insane. I needed more of her.

She clawed at my shirt, pulled the hem up and took off my tee shirt. Jeanine gazed at my chest and laid her hand on it stroking my hard muscles.

"Lord, look at you."

Her smile was the sunshine that lit my soul. For these

moments nothing dark or unholy touched me, and the rough tides that rocked my soul from the life I led eased.

"You're the most beautiful creature I've ever seen," I husked. I put my hand behind her head and urged her to lie down. Straddling her on my hands and knees, I kissed her mouth. Our tongues met and promised what was to come. Her disheveled hair and bright eyes, glowing with excitement made her beyond gorgeous. Her breasts rose and fell faster as her heart sped. My jaguar eyes sensed all, saw all, and it made me wild with need. I unzipped my camo pants and pulled them down. I wasn't wearing underwear and her lips parted slightly, indicating her desire.

"Like what you see, sweetheart?" I said. I pumped my cock a couple times with my hand and precum pearled at the tip.

Jeanine got to her knees faster than I thought she could and grabbed my length with her hand. The softness of her skin and the pressure of her small fingers on my cock made me shudder. Swiftly she put her velvet lips around the tip of my shaft, and it felt so good I could cum right then and there. Her delicate tongue fluttered against the underside of my shaft, and I groaned. Her mouth was magic, and if I let her keep this up, I'd blow in a second.

I pulled away.

"You're too good, sweetheart, and I don't want our fun to end yet. Lie down."

With questioning eyes, she did what I said, and I pulled down her panties filled with her cream. The aroma hit me, and I had to hold myself back from taking her roughly, wildly, with the abandon that soared within me. But I wanted more for her. She was unique—the woman I would spend the rest of my life with, and this first time we're together I wanted her to remember for years to come.

Not that fucking her hard wouldn't accomplish that, but I wanted her to know what was in my heart for her. The warmth there had grown from a spark to the power of the sun. I was her Earth, and I'd circle around her forever.

I pushed her legs so that her feet were flat on the ground and lowered my head to the sweetness between her legs. She was wet, and the first laps of my tongue drove more of her. I buried my face in her sweet flesh and lapped her cream. My mouth and tongue explored her intimate folds, and her hips bucked on my face. I was so lost in her that I didn't hear Kane enter the cave.

He growled with complaint like I had taken his cookie, but Jeanine only meowed. "Come here, baby," she said.

Kane padded toward her and butted his head to her face. She pulled his head down with her hands and whispered into his ear.

My teammate shifted, and naked, it was easy to see his stiff cock so hard that the vein along the side pulsed.

"Damon's been having a feast, but I need something in my mouth too," she said with a wicked glint in her eyes.

We both groaned then, but Kane was an opportunist, so he wasted no time in straddling her chest. With his back to me, I didn't see what she was doing, but her moans of enjoyment were hot, and I went back to tonguing her. She squirmed as I speared her entrance with my tongue, and the muffled sounds of her pleasure drove me wild.

Kane slid back and cried out, and I continued my assault on my lover's flesh until she cried out too. Her cream gushed on my tongue, and I lapped it up.

My teammate slid off her middle, and I saw Jeanine's chest painted with Kane's cum. Her chest heaved, and her skin gleamed with sweat.

She was fucking gorgeous.

I helped her to sit, and she pulled her legs under her. I got to my knees too.

"I need you, sweetheart."

Jeanine groaned, and I slid into her mouth. It was hot, wet, and tight, and I didn't think I would last long at all. I stilled, trying to get hold of myself, but Jeanine would have none of that. Our eyes met, and her tongue slid around my shaft. She grabbed my hips and pulled me inside until fire burned through me and I exploded.

She swallowed it all.

I kissed her hard and tasted myself in her mouth. She was mine. I pushed my hips against her and felt the tingle and pull of excitement once again.

"What's going on here?" said a gruff voice. Our heads turned to Ryker standing in the cave's entrance with his hands on his hips. Gunner stood behind him.

"Apparently proving a point," I said. "I thought you were on patrol?"

"And I thought you were keeping an eye on Jeanine. I guess we were both wrong."

"You weren't. I kept an eye on her."

"And more," said Kane in a suggestive tone.

Jeanine stared at our team leader. Of all of us, Ryker was broader and more ripped. Every muscle popped on his frame displaying the raw kinetic power of his body.

"Whoa, dude, put that weapon away." I referred to his rigid cock which was hard enough to bounce against his stomach.

"Speak for yourself," said Jeanine.

Ryker took swift steps and held his hand out to Jeanine to help her stand.

"Hey, doll. What's been going on?"

"Damon's trying to convince me I should date all of you. He thought he'd show me the value of having four men at my beck and call."

"He must not be doing a good job. You sound unsure," rumbled Ryker.

"That's a tall order."

"What makes you say that?"

"Four men? There are plenty of women who can barely handle one man."

"Let's see what we can do to convince you," said Ryker in a low rumbling voice.

Jeanine sucked on her lips, and Gunner moved to her back and Ryker to her front. He slanted his head down and kissed her hard while Gunner kissed her back and squeezed her round bottom. It was hot watching Ryker and Gunner tease her, and I got hard again watching Ryker sucking on her nipples. Gunner slid his cock between her cheeks, and she whimpered, especially when Ryker stroked her between her legs.

"Please, please," she muttered.

"Say you'll stay with us," said Ryker.

"I don't know. This is so… Oh!" Her protests were quickly quieted as her body responded.

Gunner had knelt and was now happily engaged in tonguing her rosebud. She moaned and squirmed between them.

"Fuck," said Kane. "I'm gonna cum just from watching this." His hand stroked his cock, just as mine pumped my own length. We barely gotten started and the steamy thoughts running through my brain gained speed. I was fast approaching the point where I wasn't thinking anymore. I just watched and got hotter as Ryker slipped his fingers inside her and worked them with expert precision until she screamed and bucked on his hand.

Good lord, I wanted all of them, though how could I? I always thought of myself as a one-man woman. Yet, at this moment, I needed to quench the fire running through me. I'd lost count of how many times I came, and yet I wanted more.

I don't know why Ryker kept holding back or why he asked me several times if this was what I wanted. Heat and need commanded me, and I kept saying, "Yes, please, yes."

Ryker filled me in one swift movement, and electricity ran down my spine as I wrapped my legs around his waist and begged him to take me hard. Fireworks danced behind my eyelids as his cock seared me with a burning heat. My hips jutted in time with his strokes, and I got lost in a jumble of emotion, need, and desire. Time suspended, and as I become a mass of delicious sensation climbing higher.

I burst apart and cried his name. Ryker held me tight as his thrusts stuttered, and his cock pulsed inside me. He held me as we turned on our side, and Gunner continued his assault on my back and my butt, and then he was in me after Ryker pulled out. Ryker stroked my cheek and told me how beautiful and sexy I was. This was almost too much, and I got lost again. I couldn't separate who was in me or kissing me or sucking my tits or licking behind my ear. They were all around me, and I came so many times, I lost count.

Finally, we lay in a heap, curled around each other with me in the center. I just had the hottest sex of my life, and with four men, and yet, I was calm and centered. I should feel wonton and debauched, but instead, the warm glow of love spread from each of these men and to me.

I barely knew them, but I did feel connected to them, these jaguar shifters. Whatever doubts I had about this arrangement had melted in the mist of our passion. I am part of Team Shadow, their mate, woman, whatever anyone wants to call it. I'm theirs, and they are mine.

A snap of a branch outside brought Ryker to full alert, and he shifted. It was a fantastic thing to watch, and I won't ever grow tired of it. He moved with deadly stealth to the mouth of the cave, and I'm in awe of the play of muscles under his spotted hide. He's gorgeous, and my heart swelled with pride.

Damon, Gunner, and Kane stirred and glimpsed at Ryker. Gunner and Kane shifted while Damon sat next to me.

"Here, babe," he whispered. Damon handed me a pack of wet-wipes from the pack and gave me a t-shirt. "Clean up. We have to get moving anyway," Damon whispered.

"What I need is a bath," I said.

He sniffed my skin, playfully. "I like how you smell—of sex and things."

"And things? Is this how you wax poetic?"

"Nope," he said with a grin. "I used other things for wax."

"You're so bad."

He waggled his eyebrows. "Yes. So bad I'm good."

Ryker snorted. "Okay, you guys. The noise came from monkeys moving in the canopy, but night has fallen and it's time to roll. Let's go over the plan. Kane and Gunner, you'll wear your catsuits. Kane, go to the northeast point, and Gunner, southeast." He held out one rifle to Damon. "You take point. And Jeanine, stay here."

"But—"

"No buts. You're not trained in combat, and an untrained combatant is a liability to herself and her team. You'll help us most by staying put."

I don't like this, not at all. I want to be there to look for Surma.

"No. I'll hang back, but I will not stay here."

Ryker growled, and I gathered he wasn't used to someone questioning his orders.

"Ryker," said Damon, as if appealing to his better nature.

"Chief," said Gunner. "I don't want her sitting in a cave alone."

"Yeah," said Kane. "A cave is not the best defensive position, especially if you don't have a weapon."

Ryker threw his hands into the air.

"Okay, but stay well behind me. And if you don't behave, I'll have to discipline you."

"Why," I said, "do you make that sound more fun than it should?"

The rest of the guys laughed while Ryker growled.

"Let's move out."

Ryker hefted his backpack and headed out of the cave.

"I don't understand him," I said.

Damon shrugged and then shouldered his pack and rifle. "He doesn't want you to see what we do. Someone will die tonight, and it won't be us."

"Like I don't know what it is you do."

"No, babe, you don't," said Gunner. He gave me a peck on the cheek and then shifted to his animal form. With one glance over his shoulder and what I swore was a smile on his face, he stalked into the night, and Kane followed him.

Damon put one of the backpacks on my shoulders and shouldered two. "Let's go," he said.

It was dark, the thick canopy hid the moon, and a small part of me regretted the decision to follow. My eyes weren't as good as theirs. It made sense they could apparently see better in the dark. The sounds of the rainforest assailed me, putting me on edge. The smells of rotten vegetation and the whiff of flowers floated thick in the air. The over-sweet aroma of rotting fruit mixed with mud and damp earth rose around me. Animals skittered unseen in the dark, flies buzzed, and insects hummed while mosquitoes tried to light on me. Yeah, coming along was not my best idea.

But I picked my way along the descending trail, and soon I spotted the lights from the docked boats and the buildings in the cove. Waves rolled onto the shore, and the boats rocked in their mooring. In the illumination of the lighted window, I saw a guard with a rifle backlit by lights from the window pacing the length of the building. He stiffened, apparently hearing a noise, and then disappeared around the side. He didn't return.

With the sound of crashing glass, the unmistakable outline of Aedan Morgan burst of the building, yelling in Spanish. Men ran toward him until a jaguar dashed from the building and leaped on top of him, raking Morgan's shoulders with his claws. Gunner was right. I didn't need to witness Morgan's gruesome death, and I looked away.

A rattle of gunfire peppered the night, and I looked up again to see another jaguar fly at the man shooting at the cat that downed Morgan. I put my hand over my mouth to keep from crying out. Several shots cracked the night, and the man shooting at the cat fell. Ryker stepped out of the tree line followed by Damon, and he shouted in Spanish to the half-dozen men there. They dropped to the sandy beach.

Boats at the dock started their engines and made for open water, but then a bright light burst out from nowhere, and someone spoke through a bullhorn in Spanish. My gut clenched. Who were these people? I looked to Ryker, but he didn't seem alarmed. In fact, he waved for me to join him.

I tore out of the forest and ran to Ryker. Damon took plastic strips from his pack and then searched the men lying in the sand, zip-tying their hands behind their backs.

"What's going on?" I said, looking over my shoulder to the light coming closer to shore.

"The cavalry finally showed up. They just announced that the boats should turn off their engines and wait to be boarded. If anyone tries to run, a French navy boat will wait for them outside the harbor."

I didn't understand what was going on. Damon was now questioned the men roughly. He glanced back at Ryker and me.

"The small building to the side of the bigger one," he said grimly.

"Take her," said Ryker. "I'll watch them." He pointed his rifle over the men as a large raft pulled up on the dock.

"Let's go," repeated Damon, and he took my hand. Swiftly we moved to the shed, and in the dark space between the two buildings, I spotted two sets of glowing eyes. Damon tossed two backpacks toward them.

"Dress. We have visitors."

A padlock hung on the door to the tin shack, and Damon used the butt of his rifle to break it. He pulled the door open.

Damon fumbled around inside, and a single light switched on, and my heart stopped.

Handcuffed to a pipe running along the wall slumped a

woman. She crumpled against the wall, but I recognized her face.

"Surma!"

I ran to my friend, who looked at me dully. Her beautiful dark-skinned face showed old bruises, and one eye was closed and crusted.

"I'm here, Surma. It's me, Jeanine."

Damon took the underwire from my bra and worked the lock of the handcuffs. After a few tries, the cuffs clicked open, and Surma fell into my arms.

"Jeanine?" she said.

Damon handed me a water bottle. "See if she can drink."

I put the bottle to her lips, and she took a few sips and then some more. Her eyes lost some dullness.

"How?" she croaked. "Why?"

"That I found you? It's a long story."

She swallowed. "And who is tall, dark and handsome there?"

"Mine," I said. "You can't have him."

"Should have known," she said. "I go to the Caribbean, but you end up with the hot guy."

"Well, that's another long story."

"I'll go get help," said Damon with a smile.

But before I knew it, men swept inside with a stretcher.

"If you'll excuse us, miss, we'll take it from here."

Summarily dismissed, I walked out of the shack only to find my four men lined up and scowling as a man dressed in blue camo addressed them. I stepped closer, and the man's head snapped up.

"Who is that?" he said.

"A woman on Morgan's ship," said Ryker. "We rescued her."

Ryker's voice was coldly professional, and it stopped me short. Why would he talk about me as if he barely knew me?

"Is this true, Thomas?"

Thomas? Who the hell was Thomas? Damon stiffened and spoke in the same tone as Ryker.

"Yes, Doctor Melkot."

Doctor Melkot? Not an officer? Why were the guys acting like he was their commanding officer?

"Why did you do that, Ryker? You put off everyone else."

"She got caught with us when the ship blew, sir," said Ryker. "There was no other option."

"I see," said Melkot. He scowled as if he didn't believe Ryker. What that hell was going on?

This Melkot character walked toward me, and Gunner whipped his head toward me and mouthed, "Say nothing." Gunner's worried expression set me on edge, and as the man grew closer, my heart pounded.

"Hello," said Melkot kindly. "I hear my boys found you."

His boys? From the expression on the guys' faces, I'm sure that is the last thing they wanted that man to call them.

"Yes," I said.

"And your name is?"

"Jeanine Lee."

"Sir," said Ryker. "We need to wrap up this mission and head back to base."

"Don't worry, Chief. You've done your part and most effectively. You didn't stop until you hit your mission objective." Melkot's eyes strayed to the body of Morgan splayed on the sand.

"Yes, sir," said Ryker. "Then we should head back to base."

"It's time for your physical," said Melkot. "You'll be coming with me to the facility."

"I'm sure our mission commander—"

"Okayed this physical."

"And what about Miss Lee, Doctor? We should see she

gets back home. She lost her passport when the ship blew up."

Melkot eyed Ryker with suspicion and glanced at Gunner, Kane, and Damon. Something was up and big time, but I didn't know what it was. Why had Ryker acted icily and Gunner told me to say nothing? Why did all of them look like they wanted to rip this doctor's throat out?

"Get in the raft, gentlemen. We're going home. As for Miss Lee, I'll have an officer escort her to the American consulate."

Melkot spoke to Ryker with a dismissiveness that made me want to smack him. How dare he treat this team of men, these soldiers, who put their lives on the line each day as if they were—what?

The coldly clinical eye this doctor regarded my men told me what. Lab rats. That's what he thought. Not men, but creatures to study.

They didn't look at me, which hurt me to the core. This man ordered them away from me, and they didn't stop him. I don't know what I expected. I had thought they cared about me.

They walked away without a backward glance, and at that moment, my world collapsed.

"Is there a problem, Miss Lee?" said Melkot.

"Um, no. I'm just concerned about my friend, Surma."

"And how do you know Miss Jones?"

"We went to college together. She was my roommate."

"Miss Jones will be fine. We're taking her to the ship, and she'll be cared for there."

"Oh."

"We'll get you to town and call the consulate. They'll help you get a temporary passport so you can go home."

It wasn't that easy, and I spent a couple uncomfortable hours while some men in nondescript uniforms hauled off

Morgan's body and "tidied" the beach. I didn't pay much attention because I couldn't fathom that Ryker, Damon, Gunner, and Kane had left. I didn't understand why they did, or why that doctor insisted they go with him, or if I'd ever see them again. If they disappeared in the giant maw of the black ops military machine, how could I ever find them again?

It confused me and left me distraught; a great open hole opened in my heart at once. This wasn't right. Those men were mine and had no business leaving me here on the no-name island with people I didn't know. They should have stayed with me, dammit. That's what they said, and what they insisted on, and now they weren't here.

I had never felt so alone or abandoned in my life.

RYKER

Jeanine is in my arms, and I've kissed her so many times her lips are red from the scruff of my beard. She is beautiful, and her hot channel holds me so tightly I feel every pulse of her heart. Jeanine is mine in a way no other woman has ever been, and I take her again, and again, and I never get enough of her. I gaze into her crystal blue eyes, and she smiles. Then her gorgeous face morphs into sadness and disappointment like the day on the beach when that fucking asshole Melkot forced me to leave her.

I wake breathing hard, and I concentrate on controlling it. Melkot cannot learn we've taken a mate. He would rip away her autonomy and subject her to constant tests in the name of "national security," and we could not allow that. Each of my team suffered the casual cruelties of Melkot's experiments.

As soon as we were on the raft, that bastard, shot us with tranq darts in rapid shots that took us all by surprise. As a result, I woke up groggy and disoriented in this room, pissed as hell and with nothing I could do about it. The past couple days passed with no contact with him and only food pushed through a narrow slot in the door at regular intervals.

This was Melkot's way of wearing us down. He did it often enough when we were teens, but we were grown men now, and graduates of the SEAL torture techniques class. I could withstand this even if my cat growled for its freedom. I pitied the man that opened that door because when you cage my cat, you take your life into your own hands.

The clock on the wall in my room told me it was too early in the morning to be up, at least for here. Still, I woke and used the small bathroom to shower and do the usual stuff. I don't hurry because the day would be long enough as it is.

The only easy day was yesterday. That's a SEAL truism, and we've survived hellish conditions to earn our trident, the hardware we wear on our uniforms which identified us as SEALs. The badge depicted an Eagle perched atop an anchor, a trident in one claw. The other clutches a flintlock pistol representing the sea, land, and air that makes up the environments SEALs operate in. It is the only mark that tells you someone is a SEAL when in uniform. We don't wear patches or any other badges announcing what we are.

Our code weds us to anonymity. We SEALs don't discuss our status or our missions, not even among friends and family. It's part of the reason the divorce rate among SEALs is ninety percent. How can you keep a relationship going when you can't share a huge portion of your life with your significant other?

What right did I have to claim Jeanine as my mate? What kind of life can I give her? I can't do it in uniform. Damon was right. We had to leave the service if we wanted to claim her as our mate permanently. And that bastard Melkot would never allow that.

I paced my cell. Pitted and painted white cement walls marked the four corners of my world. They reminded me of the barracks at the Marine training base at Parris Island when I went there as an instructor for a short time. The barracks were sparkling clean but carried a worn look, despite new paint on the walls, as if the despair of men training hard seeped into the walls. My room here featured a single bunk, a dented metal locker, and a simple desk and chair. A thin mattress and pillow, old sheets, a rough blanket covered the bunk and sported the same world-weariness as Parris Island.

Navy gray paint colored the cement floor. A ceiling light with a cage over the bulb and a recessed light inset in the ceiling provided the only illumination in the room. The small bathroom carried only basic toiletries—toothpaste, a comb, soap, and toilet paper. For reading material, a few worn military strategy books and a porn mag sat on the desk. Only the best for our troops. I didn't bother to look at the porn mag. Jeanine in my dreams was what made my blood run hot.

Yeah, I was in a cage, and not a nice one.

That bastard Melkot cut off my contact with my CO. He's not supposed to, but then why would he allow his prized lab rats go? Sometimes I think we're the only reason he gets such generous funding from the government. But he performed plenty of testing on us before they sent us to SEAL training. Why is he so interested in us now?

Worse yet, he's cut off access to the rest of my team. He knows how that will go. We're bonded in a way other cats are not. Melkot taught us all about cat behaviors so we could track how they manifested. We found out we had a few niggles that may result from our human DNA mixing with Jaguar. When kept apart too long, we get aggressive. The bond between us made an effective team and worked against anyone who attempted to separate us. Melkot knew this, so I have to wonder what game he's playing.

My extra-sharp hearing catches the stamp of boots coming at me. The door lock buzzed and the metal door opened.

"Chief Hardin," said the young guard. He couldn't be more than eighteen and no match for me if I took him. "Dr. Melkot wants to talk with you."

I thought briefly about refusing, but that wouldn't get my team or me anywhere. It was an opportunity to do a little recon, so I followed the guard down the halls, memorizing the twists and turns as they taught in special ops training. This wasn't the research facility I initially stayed at, and I wondered what that meant. Did Melkot get some promotion or demotion? It was hard to tell.

The guard led me to a standard office. He opened the door, and I spotted Melkot sitting behind a desk with his back to me while he looked at his cell phone. Two windows sat on opposite ends of the wall, but something glazed the glass so I could'nt see outside to get an idea of where I was. The guard shut the door behind me.

"I know what you're thinking, Ryker," said Melkot. "You're working every sense you have to divine your location. But I've planned things so you can't, so just sit down and relax. I'd like to have a little chat with you."

I stood with my hands behind my back at parade rest.

"I'll stand." I left off the "sir." He did not deserve that honorific.

He shrugged. "Suit yourself."

Melkot twisted his desk chair to face me. His face carried more age lines the last time I saw him, and his dirty blond hair had thinned. His eyes were less bright as if something washed the light from them. He was a dispirited man.

"So, I've been reviewing our files on you and your team. You have the highest mission success rate of any SEAL team. Do you realize that?"

"I guessed, yes."

"And you appreciate that you and your team are the only four jaguar shifters in the service?"

"I suspected."

"The brass would want more."

This time it was my turn to shrug.

"Since we can't find more like you, the brass wants to breed more of you."

It takes a lot to horrify me. I'd seen and done terrible things, the kind which can shrivel a man's soul. But this? This idea sent a shiver of disgust through me. One does not breed soldiers.

"We've lined up female volunteers—"

"No."

"Your participation would be minimal. The military will take superb care of the women and children."

"And I said *no*."

"You'll receive a hefty bonus for each child. If you just wish to give your contribution in a cup, we'll take that, but conception is easier if—"

Was this man insane? What caused him to assume I would go along with a bizarre plan like this? Breed Jaguar shifters to spin them into soldiers?

"More than one child is optimal. And if the bonding you share with your teammates works the same as with the children, then we need four from each man—"

"Does 'hell, no' convey the depth of my feelings in this matter?"

Melkot looked up at me with disbelief.

"I don't understand your reluctance. Neither you nor your team are monks."

"That's different. That's recreation. You're talking about taking my child and making it into a weapon from birth."

"I still don't see the problem. The military has given you a home, a purpose, and a way to contribute to your country. You should be proud if your progeny serves."

I leaned over his desk and growled which startled him. I had never displayed aggression against him until now.

"Fuck, no. Does that cover it?"

"You can run the gamut of all the swear words in the dictionary. Hell, you can add the Urban Dictionary too, but you are not leaving this facility until we get your compliance. Consider it an order from the highest levels."

I stood again at parade rest.

"That would be an illegal order. You cannot compel me or any of my team to take part in this crazy scheme. Go ahead. Keep us locked up. Keep us away from each other. You know what will happen if you do."

"Yes. That's why I ordered that you four take mess together. Go ahead, talk over the situation. Either you cooperate or grow old here."

I found it hard to believe that the brass gave us up for Melkot's crazy project. And if he thought that he'd wear us down, he was dead wrong. The doctor didn't know one crucial thing. That afternoon in the cave bonded all of to Jeanine. In no way could I share another woman's bed. And I'm sure Damon, Gunner and Kane felt exactly the same.

GUNNER

"He's a fucking idiot," said Kane.

I was glad to see my teammates. It felt like Melkot locked us up forever, though, in reality, it was a few days. Still, my inner cat coiled with nervousness. You can't keep a jungle cat locked up without serious consequences. Why do you think there are instances of zoo cats escaping and attacking people? They can't help it because their brains propel them to exercise their prey drive. And this plan of Melkot's was ridiculous.

"What made him think," I said, "that'd we'd go through with it? We couldn't—"

Ryker made a hand sign to tell me to shut it, and I got it. I wouldn't put it past Melkot to keep surveillance on us.

"I won't make soldiers for the military," Ryker said. "And I made it plain that none of us would."

"That's a given," said Damon.

"Damn straight," echoed Kane.

"Let's see if they'll let us out to play a game of basketball," said Ryker.

He wasn't talking about getting time in the yard. Over the

years we developed a code. Coupled with different covert hand signs, we could develop a strategy without our opponent's knowledge.

The code ran like this. Basketball, because of the speed of the game meant looking for the quickest option. Football was about taking the enemy head on but also timing, because football strategy mixed long and short plays for territory. Baseball was about "waiting for our pitch," waiting for the right opportunity. It also meant taking our time. Hockey meant a full-out assault, and golf signaled taking the mulligan and walking away.

"What about a game of football?" said Damon. He was best versed in tactical skills, so he was asking for Ryker's strategy.

"Nah," said Ryker. "I don't feel like twisting my knee again."

No go on "football." Ryker worried we'd get hurt or worse.

"I could go for a round of baseball," I said. "I love hitting balls out of the park."

That's me—always thinking ordinance. I told them I wanted to collect weapons first since "ball" was our code word for weapons.

"Nah," said Ryker. "I just want a quick game to work off this nervous energy."

"I don't think Dr. Meltdown will go for it," said Damon. "He's acting like a total dick toward us."

I had forgotten that Damon coined that moniker for Melkot. He did in the first few months we became a team under Melkot's supervision because he would lose it when we disobeyed him. That's when we learned how sadistic the prick was. Damon winked at us to let us and Melkot know he purposefully poked him.

"Now who's into psy-ops?" I said under my breath.

Melkot would hear that because he documented our subvocalization abilities and made sure all surveillance could pick them up.

"I'm just saying that there is no way he'll let us play basketball because he's a prick. How does he expect that we'd cooperate when he treats us like prisoners? Our instructors trained us in all torture-resistance techniques. Is he a dumbass or what? Does he really think he can overcome all the training we went through since we left the facility?"

I wanted to laugh. Damon was purposefully goading Melkot into giving us access to the outside.

Shortly after, our guards showed up at the table. We ignored them because resistance was the first tactic of all prisoners. Melkot's voice came over the intercom.

"Nice try, Damon, but I'm not a dumbass, as you succinctly put it. Back to your rooms."

"You know what?" said Ryker. "I've changed my mind. A nice game of hockey seems like a great idea right now. Suit up and play this three on one."

The look of shock and horror on the guards' faces satisfied my cat as Damon, Kane, and I shifted to our jaguars. Ryker kept his human form to explain things to our guards.

"We're leaving. Melkot tried to issue illegal orders which we will not execute. Try to stop us, and we'll treat you like any hostile force. Toss your weapons now or my team will separate you from various body parts."

The guards looked at each other, and one did not learn the SEAL truism "do not walk into your own death." He drew his weapon and fired at Ryker.

Several things happened at once. Ryker spun as the bullet hit his shoulder and Kane sprang at the shooter knocking him to the ground, and an alarm went off. Two other guards ran, which is a dangerous thing to do from a prey-driven jungle cat, and Damon ran after them. I stood my ground growling at the last guard, and he tossed his weapon then put his hands over his head. With a swipe of my dinner-dish-sized paw, I knocked him to the ground, and he stared at me in shock. I stalked toward Ryker to find he shifted into his jaguar. His shoulder bled, but his cat would heal super fast. He hissed at me, and I saw he was in shock from the gunshot. I swiped at his head, a dangerous thing to do, but it was all I could think of to snap him out of it.

No go. Ryker lunged at me as if I were the threat. We tumbled, and I shifted—another dangerous thing, but I needed my words.

"Ryker!" I yelled. "Snap out of it! We're losing our escape window!"

Kane shifted his attention from the man he injured who was squirming on the ground in pain and leaped at Ryker. This got Ryker's attention, and he released his claws gripping into my skin and jumped back.

"You clear, Ryker?" I said. "We've got to go!"

Ryker stared at me, chuffed, and then ran in the direction Damon took off in. The wound in his shoulder didn't seem to hold him back, so I figured his jaguar healing abilities had kicked in. Kane glanced at me over his shoulder then followed Ryker.

I looked at the men on the floor.

"If you try to follow us, we will kill you, understand?"

The uninjured one nodded while the other moaned and groaned. I hoped Doc Melkot had someone good with stitches here because the unlucky guard would need them.

I shifted and sped out of the mess hall toward the scent of my teammates. Several guards laid passed out on the floor, and some had visible wounds. But it struck me that for a facility this size there was a dearth of personnel. This wasn't right, and I wondered what was up.

I found Ryker, Kane, and Damon at a locked double door

at the end of the hall. Kane had shifted and worked at pulling the keypad apart. I growled, and he gave me a surprised glance. I lunged at the pad and swiped it with my claws shredding it off the wall.

"So much for finesse," said Kane. He crossed some wires, and since in cat form I couldn't see the colors, I didn't know which ones. But the door clicked open.

"The last one over the fence buys dinner," said Kane.

The klaxon continued to blare, but I saw or heard no evidence of a response. Running down another hallway brought us to another, but unlocked, double door. We pushed through it to find ourselves in an aircraft hangar, but there was no aircraft. Sun streamed in from the roof that had several missing panels. We sniffed around, each of us taking a different section. I only picked up faint traces of aircraft fuel, diesel and oil, and barely any human scent. We glanced at each other. There was something very wrong here.

Ryker padded to the side door beside the hangar door and inspected the controls for the large hydraulic door. I walked to it too and shifted. This set-up was decades old and not the current equipment in use by the military.

"What do you think?"

He sat on his haunches and gazed up at me. We both knew that tactically we couldn't stay here, but we didn't know what was out there either. Melkot could have a bunch of men out there with guns ready to take us down.

Except for a handful of guards, we hadn't encountered anything threatening - yet.

He jerked his head to the door.

"All of us out?"

He shook his head.

"Just you?"

"Yes."

"Not the best idea."

He growled, but Damon came up beside him and head-butted Ryker in the shoulder. Ryker hissed, but Damon did too. He wouldn't let Ryker go out there alone.

"All or none of us," I said. I twisted the door handle and pushed the door open, and Ryker glided out the door. Damon followed, and then Kane. I shifted one more time and followed them out even though I didn't know what we would find.

KANE

Fucking Ryker. He should have let one of us do recon, but no, he had to go out that door.

It was eerily quiet, and as I looked around, the heat, the scent of tropical vegetation and the slant of the sun in the sky told me that we hadn't gone far.

What the hell was going on?

The tarmac wasn't that large, but there was no aircraft here, and a twenty-foot-high chain link fence curiously cut off the tarmac from the hangar area. Something was very, very off. I smelled something I didn't recognize, a scent that seemed unthinking and dangerous.

Ryker roared and broke out into a run toward a section of fence that seemed shorter than the others. We got closer to the fence, but I saw it was still too high for us to jump. A normal jaguar can leap ten feet, and this was fifteen, beyond what we were capable of.

Ryker shifted and scowled.

"I don't know where the hell we are, or what this place is."

"It sure isn't an official installation."

"No, it's not, but this is our chance. No one's coming after us, so we climb."

"I don't relish the barbs at the top of that fence," I said. "And the ground appears to slope down sharply. We can't see what's below us."

"Just for that you go first and do recon." He tore off his t-shirt. "Use that."

"And mine," said Damon.

"Oh hell," said Gunner. "Take mine."

"Go," said Ryker. "That fucker Melkot is still here, and he probably has his tranq gun ready."

"He doesn't seem to be in any hurry to get to us," said Damon.

"Yeah," seconded Gunner. "Which makes me even more suspicious."

"Probably cleaning off the shit in his pants," I said cockily.

I knotted the shirts together and climbed the creaky fence. The scent of rust filled my nose, and I sneezed.

"Hurry the fuck up," said Ryker.

I flipped him off and since I was near the top, slung the shirts over the sharp barbs. It would still hurt. I had lost my sneakers in the shift, but I leveraged my right foot at the top to haul the rest of my body over the edge.

And stopped short.

"Um, guys. I know why no one is watching this fence line."

"Why?" huffed Ryker.

"Is it alligator or crocodiles in this part of the world?"

"Crocodiles," said Damon.

"Okay, there are crocs here."

"How many crocs?" asked Ryker.

"A fuck ton. Like someone stocks this moat here with crocodiles and leaves them hungry."

"They have to eat something."

"Maybe they eat each other," said Gunner.

As if to disprove Gunner's point one of the crocs ran up to the fence and hissed.

"Whoa," said Damon staring at the ugly mass of reptile.

"Someone needs to get laid," Gunner quipped.

"I don't want to be the dinner and show part of that," I said.

"Crocodiles *are* ecumenical in their diet," said Damon.

"Speak in English, you over-educated fuck," I snapped.

"They'll eat anything," said Gunner, laughing.

I'd flip off Gunner too if I didn't need my hands to balance on top of this pin cushion. Honestly, if I stayed here any longer, I'd lose the feeling in my feet.

"What do you suggest I do here, guys? Because if I stay here any longer, I'll be in the running for the longest gymnastic pose held in an escape attempt."

"Stop being a wuss," said Ryker. "You've faced worse situations in BUDs training."

"Yeah, like when you fell from that forty-foot-high rope," offered Gunner.

"Fuck you. Like you didn't whimper when they poured benzoin tincture into your broken calluses. Who was a wuss then?"

"Shit. The stuff nearly lit my hands on fire."

"In your imagination."

"Quit it," snapped Ryker. "How wide is that moat?"

"About ten feet."

"And the slope of the decline?" asked Damon.

"About thirty degrees."

"What do you think, Damon?"

"Think what?" I said.

"I think he can do it if he shifts before he does."

"Do what?" I snarled.

"Jump," said Ryker.

I was about to argue because I don't like the idea, but then I caught movement at the hangar door, and Dr. Melkot walked out holding his tranq gun.

"Go, go, go," ordered Ryker.

The others shifted and ran at Melkot, probably hoping that one would get through. I saw Melkot shooting off the gun and hitting them after another. I had no choice. If I don't get out of here, there'd be no one to help them.

"I'll be back," I said under my breath, and I coiled my muscles and jumped and shifted at the same time.

Human ancestors may have descended from the trees, but jaguars still lived in them. I sprang forward and down, catching the crocodiles' attention who churned the water in their race under me hoping to make me their next meal. I hit the edge of the moat, with several of the reptiles nipping at my heels. They followed me as I sprinted across the strip of land beyond the moat. At top speed, a jaguar can sprint sixty miles per hour, and I easily outpaced them. A shorter chain-link fence ran at the bottom of the incline, and I jumped that.

I ran, not knowing where I was going, or who I would encounter. I had to find help and get back to my teammates before Melkot shipped them off somewhere else. It's clear to me that he went rogue and probably planned on selling our children to the highest bidder. The thought made me angrier, putting speed into my paws, and I churned the ground as my claws dug in for traction. Ahead of me ran a strip of concrete, so it must be a road of some type. Roads mean civilization. To my right were mountains, and to the left more open land. Mountains meant most times, backwoods and less civilization, and clear areas pointed to water sources where people congregated, so I turned left and followed the road.

My sides ached from the exertion of running. Now a sharp pain shot through my back paw where a croc must have snagged it before I pulled away. But I would keep pushing because my team depended on me. When I found Melkot, I'd rip him a brand new asshole because a jerk like that deserves two just on general principles. It was my hate that drove me now and my concern for my teammates, and I wondered where the hell my mate was because she could be in danger too. All it took was one of us idiots to mutter her name in our sleep, and Melkot would be on her like white on rice.

The road sloped slightly downward. Down meant water, and water meant people and if I was lucky enough, I was on an island with an American consulate. The brass could disavow us, but I had to try. It was the only place where I could send a message to our central command and possibly get help. Surely, they wouldn't allow Melkot to keep us, even if it meant we'd had to spend time in the brig for fucking up.

A ramshackle building rose on the right, and then another. Many of the houses looked torn apart and then I remembered Hurricane Maria ripped the Caribbean apart. When I passed a cluster, I knew I was getting closer to the city. I thought briefly what I looked like, a jaguar running along the road, but though I heard people yelling, I was on a mission, and I wouldn't stop.

When I ran into the city proper, a police car chased me, and then another joined him, and I had to change strategy. They'd have no problem shooting a wild animal. So I found an alley with a clothesline strung across it, with clothes hung to dry. I grabbed what I could with my teeth and fled with them flapping behind me. In a darker alley, I dropped the clothes, shifted and dressed.

Every bone and muscle ached. I've shifted four times today, and I had never done that. Shifting took a tremendous amount of energy, and I was ravenous and sick to my stomach from hunger at the same time.

I sat for a few minutes, gathering my breath and my

thoughts, but soon pushed myself to my feet. I walked casually out of the alley to blend into the crowd on the narrow street. Then a gray-haired woman jabbering at me in heavily-accented English confronted me. She poked at the clothes I wore.

The policeman who had chased me earlier pulled up.

"Is there a problem?"

"Thief, thief!" the woman cried.

In a flash, he put handcuffs on me and stuffed me in the back of the police car.

"Why did you steal those woman's clothes?" asked the police officer. He spoke in English accented with a rolling rhythm as the car drove through the streets.

"Someone stole mine. I didn't want to walk around naked."

"Are you American?"

"Yes."

"And you lost your wallet and ID?"

"Yes," I said with some relief. He at least sounded helpful.

"What hotel are you staying in?"

"I'm not. I just got here, and well..."

He shook his head. "Street gangs are nasty here, like America, eh? You should know better than to walk around an unfamiliar place."

"You don't know the half of it."

"Well, you must face the magistrate, but I can arrange a phone call to the American Embassy in Barbados."

"There isn't one here?"

"Americans," he huffed. "Thinks the world belongs to them. No. Your government keeps a consulate in Barbados. That's who you must appeal to for help."

"That's fine," I said. All I needed was one phone call, and I could get the ball rolling. I hoped he hurried because there was no telling what Melkot was doing to my team.

We reached the police station, and as he led me up into the building, my head snapped up. A familiar scent reached my nose. I stared at the police desk and could not believe my eyes.

"Look, Sid," she said with her hand wrapped around the handle of a phone handset. "The police station is the only place that's letting me place calls, and that's only because if I don't get some papers, they'll jail me. They're big on immigration issues here. No, worse than that. You're my boss and you're supposed to help me. Yes, I know that I left without your permission, but this is a huge story. Yes, I've tried to reach the consulate in Barbados, but no one seems to be available. My money and my passport are in St. Lucia at my hotel. I need some money, and some help to get another passport. Yes, it's a big story, and it's all yours, but I can't write it until I get out of Dominica."

"Jeanine?"

She spun around, and her eyes grew wide. "Kane? What? Sid, I've got to go. Just wire me the money to the Western Union office, okay? Bye." She stared at me. "Why are you in handcuffs?"

"Do you know this man?" said the constable.

"Yes, he's my—"

"Husband, I'm her husband. Baby? I've been looking all over for you. Thank God you're okay."

She rushed to me and put her arms around me. "Kane, oh my God. I thought—"

"Shh, shh," I said. "It's okay now."

"Is it?"

"Not quite."

"You too?" she asked. "I can't find Surma anywhere."

DAMON

$\mathcal{A}$s we say in the Navy, "Situation Normal, All Fucked Up."

Dr. Meltdown left us in the dark in all ways possible. He knew that while we can see at night, we can't in total blackness, and he wanted to make things as uncomfortable as possible. He turned off the lights, didn't feed us, and didn't let us congregate. Melkot knew how those things would affect us. Not the dark thing, but with our fast metabolism, the lack of food was a problem. Feral is what Melkot called it, the unreasonable aggression that overtook us when our cats got angry. We could control it better than when we were teens, but worrying about the fate of Kane and Jeanine might send me over the edge. Kane could take care of himself, but figuring out Melkot was now a rogue agent made me worry about what he might do to Jeanine.

Melkot knew our ins and outs because he researched them when we were in our teens. But things changed when they sent us into the military for training. We were the youngest group there, and it was brutal. We started with an eight-week boot camp and progressed into a year and a half of different SEAL training programs designed to be impossibly difficult.

In BUDs training, our day started at 5 a.m. with a five-mile run before breakfast. The rest of the day, and half the night was one punishing physical feat after another. We all got deep cuts and calluses on our hands while brutal instructors physically and verbally abused us.

It was for our own good. But the dropout rate for that twenty-six weeks of misery can run from seventy to ninety percent. Like they said in roll call, "Look to the right and to the left, and say 'goodbye.' One of you won't be here tomorrow."

But that wasn't us, not Team Shadow. We always stuck it out because if one of us rang out, we'd all have to do the same.

And none of us wanted that.

So, I sat, and waited, and ignored the clawing hunger in my belly. I needed to see my teammates and missed my mate. I had to believe that Kane was out there getting help for us and that he wasn't lying in a ditch dead.

Okay, so I'm fatalistic when I haven't eaten. I put those candy bar commercials to shame, the ones that say, "You aren't you when you're hungry."

Footsteps walked down the hall, and I readied the home-made rope I constructed from my sheets. It wasn't easy to tear the fabric quietly. I had to sing over the sound of the sheet tearing, but then I braided the strips together and made knots through it. It was an effective weapon.

The door opened, and I covered my eyes in case they turned on the light because I didn't want to get blinded. And the light flashed on, and what, or rather who, I smelled was familiar, but I couldn't place it.

"Are you okay?"

My eyes adjusted, and I pulled my hands away and stared.

"You're Jeanine's friend, Surma."

"Yes." She swallowed hard. Though she'd cleaned up, her face still showed ugly bruises.

"Do you know what happened to Jeanine?"

"No. Do you?"

She shook her head.

"So they didn't take her on the ship?"

"What ship? It was just a stupid raft with an outboard motor. And no, Jeanine wasn't on it. Not with me."

"Fuck," I mumbled. "Do you know why you're here?"

"Morgan—he kidnapped women. A bunch, and I was one of them. He took the others someplace. I don't know. I was the last one. He waited for some doctor to pick me up.

"Melkot?"

"Yeah, that's the name. He did some tests." Surma shivered, and I felt terrible for her. Volunteers, my foot. Melkot had Morgan kidnap women for his crazy plan to breed more shifters. He probably had plans to sell the children to the highest bidders.

"What's your name?" asked Surma in a quiet voice.

"Damon."

"How do you know Jeanine?"

"I, I mean, we met her on Morgan's ship. We were doing security work for him."

"I don't remember you. I was on the yacht for a while."

"We didn't see you either. Jeanine kept asking. Morgan must have kidnapped you before we arrived."

"Yeah," she said. "That makes sense."

Her voice had a faraway sound.

"Surma, are you feeling okay?"

"No. The doctor made me take a pill. He's been giving me lots of pills, ones that make me feel like I'm burning up. I didn't want to, but he said if I did, I could eat. But instead, he brought me here."

"He's outside the door?" I whispered.

"He was, but he said he was going someplace to watch."

I almost asked, "Watch what?" until I caught an enticing scent. Her arousal hit me hard, and my cat stirred inside, restless, missing his mate. Fuck that Melkot. Why did Surma smell like this, like she was in *heat*? My cat growled within me, and restlessness filled me. I would surely take this woman but for my bond with Jeanine. No, I didn't want her, only Jeanine. Unreasonable anger stirred and shook my body. I had to do something before I lost control. I took Surma's arms and propelled her to the bathroom.

"Get into the bathroom. Lock the door. Take the longest shower ever. Don't come out of the bathroom, do you understand?"

"No," she said.

"I'm not safe to be around."

"You look fine to me."

I roared, something I rarely do, and a startled Surma shrieked and backed into the bathroom. She slammed the door, the lock turned, then clicked and the shower started.

Good.

The intercom crackled.

"This is pointless," Melkot said. "Sooner or later, you will give in."

"Sooner or later, you can go fuck yourself. I suggest sooner." I picked up the metal chair from the desk and bashed it against the speaker set in the wall. I smashed it many times until it the metal plate over the speaker dented in and the legs on the metal chair were no longer straight. Then I started on the steel door banging on it with all my strength. I didn't expect to get far, but at least I could make my point. Each strike against the door reverberated through my body, but it also created an explosively large noise. The alarm klaxon sounded. Good. Melkot got the message. I didn't care what he did to me. I would not be part of his crazy plan.

I would not betray my mate.

Footsteps came, more men than I thought that Melkot had here and stopped at the door. I stood to the side and held the chair in the air and waited.

The door opened, and I swung, only to stop suddenly. My breath hitched as I looked upon the one person I didn't expect to see.

"Damon?" said Jeanine. I stared at her. She wore a camo uniform though she had no weapons. Behind her stood Kane in full uniform and tactical gear and a group of heavily armed men.

"What are you doing here?"

"Saving your butt."

"Both of us," said Kane.

"And you allowed her to come?" I'm incredulous he put our mate in danger.

"You couldn't stop me if you tried."

"And I tried," said Kane with a smirk.

"Where are Ryker and Gunner?" said Jeanine.

"Let's get these other doors open," ordered Kane. He pointed to two men behind them who worked on the keypads on the walls and pried them apart. This seemed old-fashioned, but it was the most effective way to open the doors without the codes. Within a few minutes, the techs had the doors open.

"Are we late to the party?" said a rough voice. Gunner looked like hell. Like me probably.

"Gunner!" said Jeanine. She whirled and gave him a big hug.

"Hey, what the hell is going on here?" growled Ryker.

"Ryker!" Jeanine hugged him too.

"Hello, mate," rumbled Ryker.

I put down the chair and grabbed Kane's arm. "We will have a long talk about Jeanine being here later."

"Yes," said Jeanine with a warning in her voice. "We will."

"What's going on?" At this moment, the bathroom door opened and Surma, half-wrapped in one of my small towels, poked her head out.

"Surma?"

"Jeanine?"

Jeanine stared at me with heat in her eyes with her hands on her hips.

"Why is my friend in your room naked?"

"Don't answer that," said Kane with a smirk. "Your answer will be used against you."

"And not in a court of law," said Gunner.

She faced me with her eyes blazing. "And what about Surma?"

"Not my idea," I said.

"That's true," said Surma, who acted a good deal more sober now than when she walked in my room. "Dr. Melkot brought me here."

"Bastard," said Jeanine. "Have they gotten that creep yet?"

Kane consulted with another man, who spoke into a radio on his shoulder and nodded.

"They found him in a closet. He's in custody now," said Kane.

"Good," said Jeanine. She spun toward me. "Just what did you do to Surma?" she said fiercely.

I held up my hands. "Nothing. I swear."

"He made me go into the bathroom and shower," said Surma. By now, she had wrapped the blanket from my bunk around her.

"Was that before or after?" said Jeanine. Her eyes narrowed as she stared at me.

Gunner laughed, and then Kane and Ryker did too.

"What?" said Jeanine, whipping around to face them.

"Gentleman," said Ryker. "Our mate is jealous."

"I am not!"

I wrapped my arms around her. "Go ahead, darling," I said after breathing in her scent. "Be as jealous as you want. We can take it. We're SEALs, and we're up for any challenge, obtaining any mission objective."

"Any?" she said.

"Yes," said Ryker. "Including getting our mate home."

Jeanine pulled away. "Now wait a minute. You make it sound like you have plans for me. I have a job. And a life."

"Yes," said Ryker. "We have a lot of talking to do."

ne year later

"Okay," I said staring at my iPad, "the last client paid us, and the new client put down a deposit, so we're in good shape."

We're in the Caribbean again, even though I vowed never to come back. But we're in the U.S. Virgin Islands, miles from the island that brought us together. Not that I minded Dominica.

I'm sitting on a lounge chair at a gorgeous luxury resort. Hurricane Maria left its mark throughout the island, and the rebuilding lent to upgrading systems. The hotel chain who hired Shadow Security sent us here to install a new security system, and we traveled here, just like we'd been doing for the the past year, to take up temporary residence until our next job.

The past year saw lots of changes. The first few months were stressful, as my guys, as I call them now, disengaged from military service. The higher ups didn't like it, and the service may recall them to active duty, but officially Team Shadow now was Shadow Security Service.

Gunner pulled the iPad from my hands.

"You're looking stressed," he said. "I don't like that. And the guys won't like that."

"What am I supposed to do? How can I work from here?"

"And why can't you? We have an international phone plan and wifi. Why can't you make sales calls poolside?"

That was another change. Following Team Shadow's rescue, the Navy insisted I signed a ton of legal agreements that made it explicitly clear if I divulged any information, the punishment would be swift, severe, and swept under the rug. The biggest story of my life was a national security secret. My boss was furious with the cover story Special Ops gave me and fired me for misappropriating company funds for my "vacation." And since the media world was surprisingly small, getting a job in my former field was, as the guys say, a no-go. Fortunately, I found I had a talent for sales.

"Jeanine?" said Gunner.

"Because it's too romantic and my thoughts wander. When are you guys going to finish the work? You promised me a vacation. Some alone time? You've all been so busy."

Gunner took both of my hand and kissed them.

"We're almost done. Just another day or two."

"A day or two!"

"You tell us all the time that establishing a new business is hard work. Do some shopping.

"Why?"

"Buy a new dress."

"No. I don't need a new dress."

"Are you sure?" He smiled.

"Gunner, what are you going on about?"

"Nothing," he said.

"You're hiding something."

"Nope," he said. But he smiled, which tipped me off. Gunner's face hides little.

Gunner's phone chimed, and he looked at it.

"That's great," he murmured.

"What?"

"The Dominica justice system has spoken. They sentenced Dr. Melkot to thirty years for kidnapping."

"Wow."

"The maximum term is seven years per count, and since we found four other women besides Surma, that added up. I'm glad they aren't letting him serve his sentence concurrently."

"They let him skate on five years," I said sourly. "After what he put Surma through, he deserves every year."

"He's not a young man. He'll be seventy before he gets out."

I huffed, but he was right, I didn't have to like it.

Another text commanded Gunner's attention, and he nodded.

"Let's go," he said.

"Where?"

"You'll see."

"Is this a surprise?"

"Yes."

"I knew it. You guys have been sneaking around for days looking all suspicious."

"We do not sneak," said Gunner. "We deploy."

"And what did you 'deploy' this time?"

Gunner smiled and put my iPad in my straw bag and held out his hand.

"You'll see."

"You won't tell me, will you?"

"Nope."

I huffed, but I wasn't angry with him. I didn't know what to expect, but the guys' surprises were always fun.

But I didn't expect this.

We drove out to shore, which was a beautiful ride, and I enjoyed the sun and the wind through my hair. This was a beautiful place, paradise really. But then Gunner pulled into the driveway and stopped at the side of the house. From here, I saw the ocean, and the crystal blue waters placidly washing on the shore. The house stood two stories high, as many island homes do, with a wraparound veranda. It looked boxy from this perspective, but then Caribbean homes had more on the inside than the outside.

"Why are we here, Gunner?"

"It's kinda a party."

"What do you mean? Gunner!" I said with exasperation.

"Now keep an open mind. It's unfortunate, but Hurricane Maria opened the real estate market. And we had to do some work on it, but—"

"Gunner?"

I got out of car, and Ryker walked from inside the house onto the veranda.

"Hi, doll. Come on up."

"What did you guys do?"

"Let me show you."

I walked up the steps to the veranda with Gunner behind me.

Ryker smiled and put his arm around my waist and shepherded me into the house. There Kane and Damon stood in the kitchen. Champagne flutes lined the granite island that separated the kitchen from the large living area. Champagne chilled in an ice bucket.

"Welcome to your new home," said Damon.

"Now," said Kane, "before you say no, we got it at a great price because of the hurricane. It needed a new roof, but we took care of that right away."

"And repaired the water damage," said Gunner.

"We replaced nearly every wall," said Ryker.

"There are seven bedrooms upstairs," said Gunner, "and a small apartment downstairs we can rent as a vacation rental."

"Or not," said Ryker. "We can use it as an office."

"And five bathrooms upstairs. It should be large enough," said Gunner.

"Well, yes, that's for sure," I said. "It is. But seven bedrooms?"

"In case," said Ryker nuzzling my neck, "we want to expand our little family."

I swallowed hard. "Expand?"

"Sure. We're not going anywhere," said Damon. "And the idea of little SEALs running around has a certain appeal."

"And this way, three of us can do jobs and rotate who stays with you," said Kane.

"That is when you want to stay home," said Kane.

Home.

Why didn't it hit me before this? Was it our nomadic life-style? The going from one job to another without a break? I looked at Damon, Gunner, and Kane, all with hope twinkling in their eyes. But it hit me.

These men were my family—forever.

"Dammit," I said. "You should have talked to me about this."

"I told you," said Gunner to Ryker.

"Then we'll just have to persuade her," said Ryker. He nibbled on my neck. I can see where this is heading; right to the bedroom. While I'm not opposed, I want to make one thing clear.

"No," I said.

"What, we can't persuade you?" said Kane.

"No. You don't need to persuade me. Wherever you guys are is my home. So let's open that champagne."

· · ·

Did you love Jeanine's story? Keep the flames of love going with Jessica's story in the next book in my Fated Shifter Mates Collection, **Mated to the Pride.**

Jessica knew there had to be more to life, so on a whim she answered a newspaper ad for temporary house help. Now she's found herself drawn body and soul to her four new housemates...

MATED TO THE PRIDE

BLAKE

*O*ur pride's workout routine was always punishing, but never more so than the few weeks before a big mission. Now that there were only ten days before we left for our latest engagement, I was holding nothing back. As alpha commander, senior both in terms of our pride and military experience, it was my responsibility to keep these men alive.

Of course, I did that in many different ways — but keeping them in peak physical condition definitely didn't hurt.

I paced my breathing as I continued on the rowing machine, pushing hard to meet the same high bar I'd set for the others. Sure, we stuck to traditional pride hierarchy like any other group of shifters, but our work bound us together. I was their leader, but also their equal. I never asked them to do anything I wouldn't do myself.

"You okay there, chief?"

I paused to look across at the speaker. If I wasn't pushing my body so hard, Hale's grin would be as infectious as always. Of the entire pride, it was Hale that had the most feline energy in this form. His dark, narrow eyes were intense and focused, playful as he was. Outsiders tended to find him intimidating and were surprised to learn that we didn't agree often — especially since Hale was also my second-in-command.

I shot him a look back. "I'm fine."

"I don't know. You got some heavy breathing going on over there."

I shook my head. I was too focused to smile, but Hale knew me well enough to read it in my eyes. "Focus on yourself, smart-ass. You sure you haven't turned down the resistance?"

"I just want everyone to know," said Hale, turning around to face Stone and Preston, "that our fearless leader is accusing me of slacking off."

"Uh-huh," said Preston. He wasn't much of a talker, but he didn't have to be. The smirk he shot back at Hale did all the talking for him. Strangers tended to be confused by that. They hadn't learned to pick up on his signals like we had and saw him as a mystery man. An enigma. The piercings in his upper ear and eyebrow likely helped that along — as well as his sleek wave of dark hair, dashed with flecks of premature silver. Preston was only 28, and looked it. The little gray looked curious, and often had people joking that we put him through too much stress.

"If only he could accuse you of shutting up," said Stone.

"Wow," Hale shot back. "I resent that."

Like Hale, Stone was never too tired to smile, and had a playful look even now as he pushed hard through the rowing motions. These youngest two members of our pride, Stone at 26 and Hale at 27, were always batting friendly insults back and forth between one another. At 30, I wasn't much older, but I still didn't know where they got their energy from.

Maybe my mind was just occupied with more serious things.

"How much time left?" Stone asked.

"One more minute," I said. "Then we run."

"Thank fuck." Stone pressed on, lifting a hand to push back the bleach-blond sweep of his hair. Needless to say, that bleach-blond was the subject of a lot of Hale's teasing, but nobody could deny that it suited him. As alpha of the pride, I kind of had to appreciate that at least one of us was sporting something like a mane in human form.

It wasn't exactly the most practical haircut for paramilitary operations, but Stone was our medic. I figured I could cut him a little slack.

When the timer finally hit zero, the room gave a collective exhale. All the tension in our muscles faded away to sweat and heat, and there was a fizz of relief in the air as we headed outside.

"Good work today," I said, pausing to pat Preston's shoulder as he passed, and closing the door behind us. "I didn't hear too many complaints. Everybody had good form. Shaping up pretty well for next week."

"If we're not exhausted," said Hale, rolling his shoulders back. "Shit. I wish my lion wasn't so ready to go right now. I want to fall down face-first into a snack."

"You always do," Stone teased. "C'mon. Let's get this over with."

As he reached the edge of the gravel path outside our home, he shifted in the blink of an eye. Where there had once been lithe limbs and tan skin, Stone was now all sand-colored fur — the well-shaped, muscular form of a lion's body, paws pounding against the floor hard enough to leave imprints in the crumbly earth.

The rest of us followed close behind, keeping pace with our medic. Even your average human could probably spot the difference between us, but it was even easier for our pride. Stone's blond hair seemed to be reflected in the lightness of his mane, and how it so closely mirrored the rest of his fur. Flecks of gray were peppered through Preston's dark, near-black mane. Hale stood taller than the rest of us, and with a reddish sheen to him that was absent from his human form. As for me, I was a muddy gray with a mane that lightened at the edges, with muscular limbs that marked me out as leader.

Of course, human eyes wouldn't catch all these details at first glance. For one thing, we were moving quick enough to be easily missed, dust whipping up around us in a storm. After working our human bodies so hard today, this felt like a treat. Like the best kind of cool-down stretch. We wouldn't feel like ourselves if we had no time to do this. Our human forms were fine, but there was something pure and right about this form that we needed every once in a while. However the others experienced it, I could feel the earth pulsing through my paws, connected to me in a way that my other shape wasn't.

We could communicate differently as lions, too. We didn't need to speak to fall into formation, forming a chain that worked perfectly as we made our way through the undergrowth and the tightly-packed forest. We each took turns in the lead, fast and furious as we coursed over gulches and dips in the ground. It was seamless. Nobody had to snarl or roar to advertise their position; we were just aware of each other, as easily as we were aware of ourselves. We barely had to think about it.

This innate sense of flow and cooperation was why we worked so well together as a military unit. Maybe our commanding officer didn't really understand what bonded us so closely. Our shifter status was highly classified information. Still, it was obvious to everyone who came into contact with us how useful our unspoken communication could be in any intense and difficult situation.

This was why we were trusted with such important missions. This was why we were being sent away in ten days. No amount of physical aptitude or training could compare to the kind of team that we had — and our physical skills were top-notch in any case.

It was a tough life. We worked hard, and had little time to ourselves, but the pride kept each other sane and happy. There'd be time for fun and settling down later in our lives.

Probably.

By the time our lion muscles were as exhausted as our human ones, the sun was just about to come down. I took the lead again as we headed back home, feeling the earth cool underneath our paws, and only shifted back again as we reached the yard.

I opened the door, glancing over my shoulder at the sound of Hale's yawn. He had already shifted back, stretching his arms with a slight grimace. "Man. Hard work today. I needed that run."

"I think we all did," I agreed, holding the door open so that each one of them could pass — first Hale, already yawning again, and then Preston with Stone behind him. "But we'll be grateful for being in the best possible shape when we're out there in Sigma territory."

"Damn right."

We flopped onto the long angular couch, big enough to hold us all with a little extra space… as humans, at least. Even draped over these soft cushions, ready to be lazy for the rest of the day now, I could see the strength in my pride's arms, and I knew we were ready. I had faith that not only were we likely to succeed in this mission, but it'd be over quickly and safely.

Still, there was one thing left to discuss before we started our final preparations.

"Guys," I said, glancing over my shoulder. "This place is a dump."

I was only barely exaggerating. As we'd been training so hard, the kitchen had been used to prepare several meals that hadn't quite been cleared away yet, and there were piles of clothes dropped all over the floor from where tired lions had abandoned their human things and never come back for them. Our enhanced shifter senses weren't much of a good thing when you could smell dust in the air, and see crumbs that needed lifting from the carpet all the way across the other side of the room.

This... would not work for our mission.

"We've got time yet to clear it up," said Stone, smoothing the suede of the couch arm all in the same direction. "Really shouldn't take that long."

"Uh-huh," I said. "But we can't have the cabin like this in Sigma."

Preston wrinkled his nose. "Huh. Yeah."

"It's a distraction," I said. "And clearly we've been focusing pretty hard on other things the past week or so. The work-load isn't going to be lighter once we're actually out there. Maybe we need to work something out."

"What, like a rota?"

"Hale," said Stone, eyes bright, "we all know you'd never stick to a rota."

"Actually," I pressed on, before Hale could bite back, "I was thinking more like external help. Somebody we'd bring along specifically to take care of the cabin for us."

"A shifter?" said Preston.

I shrugged, considering it. "I don't know. It could be hard to find somebody in time now. It's so last-minute. I think we're going to have to put an ad out in the paper and hope for the best. Maybe go through an agency if we absolutely have to, but… I'd prefer somebody we can approve of ourselves."

"That would be my concern," said Hale, wearing his serious hat for once. "We need somebody trustworthy, and also who understands that the place we're going is not exactly safe. That they need to take any instructions we give them seriously."

"We could interview for that," I agreed, nodding. "Stone? Preston? What do you think?"

"The budget allows for it," confirmed Stone, finally looking up from his cell phone screen. "We have a surplus. I think you're right; I think it makes sense."

"We're going to have to be careful," said Preston. "If they're not a shifter. If they don't know…"

"It wouldn't be the first time we had to keep the secret," Hale pointed out. "We could shift back before we got to the cabin every day."

"Would it be harder to make sure we're not followed, that way?" Preston folded his arms, brow furrowed in concentration as he tried to answer his own question. "I'm not against it. Just want to make sure we're doing the right thing here."

"Let's think about it," I suggested. "We can put out the ad and see who shows up to interview. Trust our instincts. If somebody fits, we'll make it work. If they don't…"

"We teach Hale how to follow a rota," said Stone, dodging as Hale tried to swat his arm.

We had a plan. Now, it just remained to be seen whether it would actually work out for us or not — and if this was really a good idea.

I sipped my coffee as I headed out of Starbucks, even though it was still a little too hot. The barista was so busy it appeared she would run off her feet, but she seemed to like her job a hell of a lot more than I liked mine. I checked my watch, picking up the pace to make sure I reached the station in time to catch the next train home.

I didn't want to spend a single minute more away from home. Today had really taken it out of me.

You would think that sitting behind a desk all day would leave you pretty well-rested, but it was actually the exact opposite. The more time I spent cooped up and staring at expense reports on a computer screen, the more I wanted to run out of that place and never look back — not that I had the energy to run.

The pay was okay. The benefits were reasonable. The commute was long, but it could be a heck of a lot worse.

But didn't I deserve something a little bit more than *okay*?

It felt like I spent most of my life working. A few years ago, I'd left college believing that my life was just about to kick into high gear. Now, I barely saw the friends I'd made there, who I'd felt so close to back then. None of us ever seemed to have time off that coincided. My life had turned into the kind of treadmill I'd only seen in movies and 'before' pictures.

I needed an injection of something good and different. Fast.

Once I finally got a seat on the train and could settle down with my coffee and my evening paper. At first, having no internet on the train felt strange but once I got used to it, I realized it let me disconnect a little from the constant barrage of social media and notifications. Now, grabbing a paper soothed me as I fell into my usual routine. I scanned the Missed Connections section first, always hoping in vain that some Prince Charming or other would have seen me across the counter at Sbarro and fallen head over heels in love with me. It could happen, right? But for some reason, there were no notices that fit my description today — just like every other day.

Never mind. On to the classified ads.

A couple of people were selling pure-breed puppies. If my apartment allowed pets, I might have considered it, but… the thousands of dollars these breeders wanted to charge didn't sit well with me considering all of the dogs that needed adopting at rescues and shelters. Somebody wanted five hundred bucks for an old couch. Judging by the attached picture, it might be worth that if it had four hundred hidden under the seat cushions. I mean, what kind of person pays to advertise an old, beat-up couch these days? Isn't that just throwing good money away?

There really wasn't much of interest today. I was about to close the paper and go back to daydreaming with my coffee when my eyes caught on a job advertisement.

Live-in home manager wanted, it read. *Competitive pay. Join our tight-knit team in a remote location for a full three-month term, with a near-immediate start. Duties will include cooking, cleaning and general home maintenance. All applicants welcome to interview — good personality fit required. Call for details.*

There was nothing special about it. It certainly wasn't my area of work. I studied finance at college, and now I stared at facts and figures all day, preparing detailed cost breakdowns along with profit and loss reports. I could cook and clean, of course, but I'd never considered doing it for a living. Not even slightly.

So why was I itching to call that number?

My fingertips hovered over the ad. Could it be that I was just lonely? They mentioned a tight-knit team, which would be a far cry away from the cut-and-dry environment of my office, where nobody exchanged more than a couple of sentences with one another. Either that, or it could be the thought of getting out of the city for a couple of months.

Now that the idea had wormed its way into my head, I couldn't shake it. The feeling was surreal. I had never even thought about leaving my job before, at least not in a serious way. Now here I was feeling drawn to a random ad in the paper that wasn't even a good fit for my expertise. Whatever 'competitive pay' meant, could it really compete with my current salary for my highly-trained job?

I dropped the paper to my lap, frowning down at my coffee. I was probably just tired. I needed to get home, make a quick dinner and binge something on Netflix. If I needed to call that number and set up an interview just to scratch the itch, then so be it. It didn't mean I had to *go through* with the interview, never mind accept the job.

Man, scratch 'make a quick dinner'. I needed takeout tonight. That much was for sure.

~

When I found myself in an Uber pulling up to a big house outside the city at 5:30pm the following day, I could barely believe I had come this far. Surely I wasn't *really* going to leave my safe, secure office job for this opportunity, no matter how well the interview went? I was probably just setting myself up for an hour of awkwardness and a pointless rejection.

All risk, no reward.

"Alright," said my Uber driver Shanice, giving me a big cheery grin as she pulled to a stop. "Here you go. Don't look so nervous, okay? You're going to do great."

"Maybe."

"Hey, none of that," she said, wagging a finger at me. "You made a great impression on me. I'm sure they're going to love you. And if you figure out you don't want the job, then… at least you don't have any regrets, you know? You took your shot. That's what life's all about."

"You're adorable," I said, although privately I couldn't help but feel like I needed to stop telling my life story to every friendly stranger I met. Shanice was cool, but she probably didn't want to know about my unnecessary job interview woes. "Thanks for the pep talk. Have a good day!"

I watched the car pull away. I wasn't a nervous person, but I couldn't help chewing the inside of my lip as I walked up to the front door of this house. It looked like a nice place. The advert was asking for a 'good personal fit'. If the people who lived here were really well-off, chances were that I wasn't going to be on their level. I lived paycheck-to-paycheck, pretty much.

Still, I had no choice now. Shanice was already halfway down the street.

I plucked up my courage and rang the doorbell.

When the door opened, I was immediately glad I hadn't run away prematurely. The guy who opened the door was…

well, *really* hot. My first thoughts didn't get any more eloquent than that. I forced my mouth into a smile so that my jaw didn't drop open, and held out my hand,

"Hi," I said, hoping my blush was light and rosy and not completely humiliating. "I'm Jess Dorsey. I'm supposed to be here for an interview, though I think I'm a little early."

"Don't worry about that," he said. When he took my hand, I felt his grip strong and serious around mine. His hand was huge, and his jaw so firm and square that it looked like somebody had cut it that way on purpose. "It's great that you're here. Come on through. And, uh. Sorry about the mess. I swear it's not usually this bad."

"Hey, no problem. That's what you're advertising for, right?"

"I think this is beyond the scope of one person's daily duties," he said, throwing me a sheepish look over his shoulder. God, he had a handsome smile. "We've just been a little busy getting ready for our trip, that's all. It's kind of piled up. I'm Hale, by the way."

We stepped into a living room space, with a huge corner couch and huge bay windows. Of course, the room wasn't really what I paid attention to — because as well as Hale, there were three other intimidatingly good-looking men scattered around the place.

Holy shit. What is this place and how do I get a membership...?

"Alright," said Hale, clapping his hands together. "Jessica. Like I said, I'm Hale. This is Preston, with the piercings. Stone's the bottle blonde."

Stone threw him a withering look and shook his head at me. "The shit I get from this guy," he said. "You wouldn't believe."

"And I'm Blake."

My eyes shifted away from Stone's easygoing smile to a much more serious face. His deep grey eyes seemed to carry a lot of weight, and his dark, short-shaven hair had a pretty military aesthetic. All this, and he also had muscular arms even thicker than the rest of his colleagues. He looked almost dangerous. The kind of guy you'd like to have on your side, and definitely wouldn't want as an opponent.

"We appreciate you coming down here on such short notice," said Blake, gesturing at an armchair that sat beside the couch. I dropped down into it, trying not to look nervous or outnumbered — though of course, I definitely was outnumbered. "We know it's a fast turnaround. We really should have started looking a long time ago, but… as you can see, we haven't been fully organized for a little while."

I smiled, appraising the room around me. It was a little messy, sure, but nothing too heinous. I didn't feel uncomfortable, or felt like I'd need to take a shower as soon as I stepped outside. "It's not so bad," I insisted. "Hale was telling me that you've been pretty busy getting ready for these three months away."

Blake nodded. "That's right. And we'd like to tell you more about that, but… before we do, I just want to point out that what we do is pretty serious work. It's classified, and we'll need you to sign non-disclosure forms and complete background checks if everything works out."

"Don't worry about all that," Stone advised. "It's just government rules. If we trust you, we trust you. We like to think we're pretty good judges of character."

I nodded, taking it all in. "I understand. It's fine with me, anyway. I've got nothing to hide."

"Open book, huh?" said Stone.

I smiled, spreading my hands. "What can I say?"

Casual as I was acting, this was all very strange. Government rules. Classified. Maybe the 'military' feel I had detected on Blake wasn't far off the mark. What exactly had I walked into?

"You wouldn't be doing anything dangerous yourself, of course," Blake continued. "What we described in the ad is exactly what we're looking for. While we focus on the reason we're out there, you'll be helping us by keeping everything running smoothly in a domestic sense."

"Right," I agreed. "Making sure there's food on the table and clean clothes to wear."

"Honestly, we're not real fussy," Hale added. "We're not going to expect shiny sinks and three-course dinners. Probably, we'll be able to take care of a lot of things ourselves. We just want to make sure we've got you there to handle the basics if we're pulling really long hours."

"I get you," I said. "That makes sense."

My eyes flicked over the four men again. Stone seemed the least scary, but he was still the kind of model-pretty you'd follow right away on Instagram. The one with the fleck of premature grey in his hair and the ear piercings — Preston? — hadn't spoken at all, but he was definitely paying attention. I felt he was observing me, not in a creepy way, but it still made me a little hot under the collar. I hoped those blue eyes found that I was up to par.

"We're leaving exactly one week from now," said Blake. He spared a glance at each of his colleagues, then turned back to me. "Since the location is classified, you'll need to travel with us, and we really would need you to stay for the full three months. Could even be longer, depending on how things go for us. Will that be okay with you?"

I nodded, listening. Then I realized something.

"Oh. Does that mean I got the job…?"

My cheeks flushed. That was quite an assumption to make, but something in the tone of his voice sounded like he was making an offer — not checking, just in case. I looked at each of the team members again, hoping I hadn't made a fool of myself.

"If our terms work for you, and you're still interested," said Blake, with a little smile. "Then yes. We'd love to have you join the team."

I flushed. They hadn't even discussed it. How could they possibly know that I was the right person for the job? But despite the fact that this didn't make sense, I couldn't fight the happy feeling that was flooding through my chest. As certain as I had been only twenty minutes ago that this was a pointless endeavor, I was thrilled.

Sure, a small part of me screamed rhetorical questions to myself like, *are you crazy?* They just told you almost nothing about the assignment except that it's secret, you won't know where you're going and that you're committing to spending three months living with them and you're going to say yes?!

But the pull of freedom from the mind-numbing monotony of facts and figures in a senseless job couldn't be denied. Saying no to this opportunity meant I'd resigned myself to feeling unfulfilled. It was less about the job and more about me. Hopefully one week's notice would be enough.

If not, well... tough.

"I'd be happy to," I said despite myself, feeling the hair on the backs of my arms stand up. This was sheer madness, but at the same time, it felt so *right*. "Thank you so much. I'll start making my preparations right away."

My Uber driver on the way home wasn't nearly as talkative. It was then that I realized I hadn't even asked about the pay. No wonder they offered me the job on the spot. They probably thought I was the dumbest candidate they'd seen — but even so, I still couldn't bring myself to regret accepting their offer. Something felt *good* about that group of men, even beyond how painfully attractive they were. I couldn't quite put my finger on it yet, but... hey.

I was about to have three whole months to work it out.

Warlock's Claim

Historical Paranormal Romance

Epic World Building Academy Romance

Reverse Harem Escapes – Great for a Quick Roll in the Hay with None of the Guilt